Tony Saint was born in Northumberland in 1968 and educated at the taxpayer's expense. In 1993 he joined the United Kingdom Immigration Service where he worked for ten years before leaving to write *Refusal Shoes* (Serpent's Tail, 2003), based on his experiences. This was followed by *Blag* in 2004. Tony has written extensively for radio and TV and is currently working on a television film about the early career of Margaret Thatcher. He has also contributed to many of the UKs national newspapers. He is married with two children and lives in South London.

Praise for *Blag*

'The novel is an eye-opener' ***Uncut***

'The absurdity and petty injustices brought Kingsley Amis to mind' ***Daily Telegraph***

'Like the novels of Magnus Mills and the TV work of Ricky Gervais and the *League of Gentlemen* crew, this is a work in the emerging school of the new absurd, the British banal – morally accurate, spiritually depressing and vastly readable' **4-star review in *Big Issue in the North***

'A very dark, fast-moving story of scam and counter-scam which doesn't pull its punches when it comes to the frailties and absurdities of immigration control – or perhaps that should be out-of-control' ***Birmingham Post***

'*Blag* is an eye-opening account of the immigration business, full of home truths likely to upset anyone, no matter what side of the immigration debate they are on' ***Buzz***

Praise for *Refusal Shoes*

'A gloriously entertaining satirical thriller' ***Guardian***

'So successful in its depiction of the flickering-fluorescent petty-politicking of immigration officers – where productivity is measured in "refused leave to enter" stamps – that you almost start worrying whether your own papers are in order' **Tony White**

'A high-farce, fast and funny debut thriller…When you take this book on holiday, get someone to bring it back for you through customs' **Arnold Brown**

'A brutally funny first novel which refuses to pull any punches' **Ben Richards**

'*Refusal Shoes* comes on like a cross between *Airport* and *League of Gentlemen*… Saint writes some very funny dialogue and offers sharp observation' ***Independent on Sunday***

'A gruesomely comic account of an immigration service… *Refusal Shoes* brings a new perspective to a big current topic while also being highly entertaining' ***Daily Telegraph***

'Part thriller, part exposé, *Refusal Shoes* is refreshingly politically incorrect and wickedly funny' ***Observer***

'*Refusal Shoes* is an amusing satirical thriller that provides an eye-popping glimpse behind the immigration desks at Heathrow. It shocks in more ways than one' ***Sunday Telegraph***

THE
ASBO
SHOW

TONY SAINT

First published in 2007 by Serpent's Tail,
4 Blackstock Mews, London N4 2BT
website: www.serpentstail.com

Typeset by Martin Worthington
Printed by Mackays of Chatham

10 9 8 7 6 5 4 3 2 1

THE
ASBO
SHOW

PROLOGUE

Merrion's quick walk turned into a limping jog as he neared the end of the long corridor, his steps snapping like whip cracks against the hard floor. Underneath his dinner jacket, the blood that had soaked his shirt had dried to a pliable crust. His hands were still sticky with it. He wondered if there was blood smeared on his face as well. That might explain the looks of oncomers who pushed themselves against the wall as he passed.

He reached the annexe to the office at the end, where the councillor's secretary sat. She rose as he entered, eyes wide, but Merrion put up a hand.

'I'm not going to hurt him,' he said.

He walked to the door, opened it and went in.

Pease sat behind a large desk, scanning a series of overlapping papers on his desk. Spreadsheets, Merrion thought, remembering one of Spence's comments.

Once in the room, Merrion halted halfway between the door and the councillor, breathing hard.

Pease looked up at him, saw the blood, thought for a moment.

'I have a police delegation arriving at any moment. Do you wish to speak to them?'

Merrion took a step forward.

'Goossens,' he said, gasping. 'It has to come down.'

'Come down?'

'It's... before somebody else gets... I started it, but look, it all got out *of hand... '*

Pease couldn't resist a look down at his figures. Merrion moved quickly to the desk and slammed both fists down.

'You have to demolish it. I'm not joking. You have got to tear the fucker down!'

Pease sat back in his chair with a sudden sense of ease, holding a pencil at each end and twirling it quickly. 'And tell me,' he asked. 'Have you fully costed this proposal?'

PART ONE

1

FOUR MONTHS EARLIER

Driving through the sequence of pointless concrete tunnels that took you west, it dawned on Roger Merrion that the news of his father's death wasn't affecting him in the way he had expected. In the way he had wanted. He felt unchanged. The ache in his shoulder was still there and he drummed the steering wheel with that familiar feeling of restlessness, the one he'd had for thirty-seven years.

He was thirty-eight next month.

In the passenger seat next to him sat Spence. He was dressed, as usual, in a blue cotton shirt, a navy blazer with silver buttons and a pair of cream chinos, painstakingly creased down the centre of each leg. The creamy smell of his aftershave Roger found oddly reassuring. He might have put on a few pounds over the years since they'd both joined the council Housing Department on virtually the same day twenty years ago, but Spence was still Spence, whatever you thought of him.

It was equally standard for Spence to be on his mobile phone these days, and he was still involved in a conversation he'd already been having when Roger had picked him up ten minutes earlier, from outside the sole bank in the city's modest Chinese quarter.

Spence had been pretty cool so far, but he was starting to get a bit narked.

'Darren. Darren, mate, I just need you to keep on top of this for me... I know... I know he's got an attitude. I told you he had an attitude. Don't let him... Listen, it's easy. Can you give him the third pallet...?'

He raised a hand and interrupted Darren in his reply.

'Darren. Just answer. Can you give him the third pallet...? Fine, then let him have the fucking thing... I know that's what we said but if he wants and you've got, why don't we all take the path of least resistance...? Yeah,' he said quietly, turning slightly into the window. 'Of course you're in for the third pallet... yeah, same cut as the others, I'll even round it up to the nearest fifty, how's that? All right, then... He's saying what?... '

Coming off the dual carriageway Roger swooped down to a roundabout offering a number of alternatives. Right was the coast, left was the retail estate featuring the new PoundBlaster megastore, less a hypermarket than a corrugated cathedral. Straight over was the Gildenhall Estate, a few square chimneys visible over a brow. A couple of smaller exits promised to lead you off somewhere different – exotic, green – but Roger had been stuck here all his life. He knew that they were a tease, that you drove along them with nowhere to turn off until they led you to a mirror-image roundabout on the opposite side of town.

He crossed the roundabout and headed for the Gildenhall Estate.

Spence had taken to rubbing his brow in exasperation.

'Darren, Darren, tell him they're paving stones. Tell him they're fucking pav... No, tell you what, Darren. Put him on. Put him on the phone, will you?'

Driving along the treeless streets, the sky apparently swooping in on him, Roger admitted to himself that the Gildenhall was a tricky estate to date without specific knowledge. A gridiron of brown, squat houses in their own grounds and three-storey blocks with flat roofs, it could either have been a post-war attempt at a cheap garden suburb or a 1970s experiment in campus lifestyle. Whatever aspirational trend it had owned on the drawing board, now it boasted the designation of 'problem locale', not of the first rank but certainly making a name for itself.

Spence's new interlocutor had come on the line.

'Funsize? Funsize, that you? How are you, son?... No, no... Come on, he's just doing his job... I know that, but three pallets is all we can give you... They're council property, mate. They're needed for, you know, wheelchair access or whatever...'

Spence lowered his window a couple of inches.

'Funsize? Tell me, how much are you paying for the slabs? No, remind me, what price are you getting on these fucking slabs?... Exactly... I know that some of them are broken and that's in the price... You've got three pallets, for God's sake. How big a back yard does he want? Don't answer that... Well, I dunno, do him some crazy paving... No, it's back in. Deffo. I saw a bloke doing it on BBC2. They've got a Latin name for it now... Yeah, crazy paving. It's the new decking,' he suggested, rolling his eyes. 'So we're sorted?...'

Having turned on to the right street, Roger slowed the car to a halt. Spence tried drawing the call to its close, leaning forward ever further as he did so.

'Right, no, that's right... That's what he... Ha ha, right... What's that? Concrete? No, can't do concrete. You'll have to go to HomeBlaster for that... I said get it there. I didn't say buy it there... Ha ha... Yep, you do that... all right, all right, mate... yeah... all the best... will do... yeah... God bless again. Bye.'

He hung up, sitting right forward, his head by this time pressed against the glove compartment, and uttered a low groan.

'Jesus,' he said, pulling himself straight. 'Some people.'

'One deal too many?' Roger asked, realising that it sounded a little pointed.

Spence just shrugged. 'I don't know. You'd think a guy who was getting company paving stones for next to nothing...'

Roger interrupted him.

'I don't want to hear any details.'

Spence clicked his tongue. 'Don't you start.'

'Come on, Spence. Hear no evil, speak no evil. That's my motto.'

Roger had time for Spence, liked him even, but he, Roger, felt the need to be circumspect. After all, he had more to lose from too intimate a knowledge of Spence's dodgy business dealings.

Roger had a wife and kids he had to think of.

Spence acted a little peeved.

'Best-quality slabs,' he muttered. 'You try and do someone a favour...'

Roger smiled. Favour was Spence's euphemism of choice for what he spent most of his time at. Wheeling, dealing, selling off spare council plant and equipment, creaming off a healthy share of the council tax slosh. And earning way more than Roger could ever imagine, even though their monthly council wage slips were virtually identical.

Spence remembered something. 'Hey. I should have said. I was sorry to hear about your dad.'

Roger nodded once with seriousness to express his thanks for the sentiment. 'I've got to go to the home this afternoon, pick everything up,' he said as they stopped at some lights. Stretching upwards, he inspected his eye closely in the rear-view mirror. 'Fucking conjunctivitis,' he muttered.

Spence looked up. 'He died of conjunctivitis?'

They both snorted with laughter, Roger glad for a sense of relief.

'No. I've got conjunctivitis.'

'That's highly fucking contagious. You should be on the Tom and Dick with that.'

'What? And waste a sickie?'

Spence had to acknowledge Roger's point, but he still looked unhappy.

'I don't want to catch it off you.'

Roger shook his head, turned up one corner of his mouth.

'I'm just feeling a bit run down. That's what it is.'

'You want to wangle a compassionate day or two.' He thrust out his bottom lip and scratched a mark on the plastic dashboard.

'I think sometimes it's better to just come to work.'

'If you say so,' muttered Spence, bending forward to get a view of the neighbourhood through the windscreen and then sitting back and stretching his arms upwards with a dramatic groan. 'What in the name of shite are we doing here?'

Roger shrugged. 'Out and about. Fresh air.'

'Do me a favour. Serving orders? I ask you.'

'Come on, Spence. You've done, what? Nine months?'

'Eleven months.'

'Eleven months. How many orders have you served in eleven months?'

'Absolutely not the point. They've got the others for that. If I start serving orders, what's that maniac Fitch going to do? They're going to give me more orders to serve. It's like a... I don't know, self-fulfilling prophecy or something.'

'Or something.'

'Look. I didn't join the Antisocial Behaviour Unit so I would actually come face to face with it. And neither,' Spence added, pushing his head back against the rest and jabbing a thumb in Roger's direction, 'did you.'

'What's that supposed to mean?' Roger asked, unable to suppress a smirk.

Spence fired a single laugh out through the sunroof.

'Ha! The balls of the man! Roger Merrion. Goes where the work isn't.'

Roger laid on the bogus effrontery. 'I don't know what you mean. I did ten years in Housing.'

'Then you got wise. Every time...' Spence slapped his own palm. 'Every time they set up a new department, who's the first person to apply? Community Liaison? Poll Tax Defaulters? And now this?'

'I like the variety.'

'You're a lazy bastard. Don't get me wrong. I salute you for it. You're my fucking hero.'

Spence was right. Of course he was right. Roger was the set-up king. Join a new section when there's bugger all to do and bale out at the first rumble of work from over the horizon. A simple enough strategy, aided by the perception around the Town Hall that Roger was, if nothing else, willing.

'Like I'm the only one,' he muttered.

Spence took this as proof of victory. He gestured down at an A4 envelope resting in the pouch on the inside of Roger's door.

'Come on, then,' he said. 'Who's the knacker in question?'

Roger passed the stuff over. Spence pulled out an orange file and another, smaller, envelope. He opened the file and speed-read the first few pages, choosing to enunciate some of the key words in a low monotone.

'Graffiti... vandalism... in-tim-i-da-tion... nothing people weren't doing twenty years ago. Fifty years ago.'

He snapped back to the inside cover.

'Sixteen,' he commented on the subject. 'Sixteen. How old's your lad now?'

Roger raised his eyebrows. 'Same. Same-ish. Fourteen.'

'What's he getting up to?'

'Nick's a smart lad.'

'Too smart to get caught, you mean.'

Spence peered inside the smaller envelope.

'So that's it?' he asked. 'That's the order?'

Roger nodded. Spence took it out and had a look at it.

'Oof,' he winced. 'They are going to just fucking love this.'

Roger had parked about three houses away from where they were calling. This was by design. It meant that you weren't likely to be seen in advance but you were still close enough to make a quick exit if things got a little tasty.

Things had been known to get a little tasty. They were getting tasty with increasing regularity.

Once out of the car, they moved quickly towards number 24, Spence going on ahead by a few strides. Having read the order, he had decided that he wanted to do the actual serving. This was Spence all over. It wasn't just about showboating, although that played a part. It was about staying in charge, keeping things moving. Spence liked to get on with it. Most of the other members of the unit liked to do the serving as well, but health and safety regulations meant you had to go in twos. Roger, the joke went, preferred to watch. Like all the best jokes, there was more than a hint of truth in it.

They passed number 22, all its windows boarded up and a green plastic bathtub planted vertically in the garden space. The Dadaist tendencies of the local yobs were starting to achieve full expression on the Gildenhall. Spence had noticed this point on the route map before. They were experimenting with pointlessness and liked it. Now it would simply be a question of the scale increasing. A concrete post dropped on to a car roof or a hijacked ambulance driven into a bus stop. No doubt about it, the Gildenhall was up and coming.

Roger blinked hard. The cold air was stinging his bad eye, making it water. He had to stop and wipe it with the cuff of his shirt. By the time he could see clearly again, Spence was at the front door of number 24, rapping hard on the plywood, even kicking it once to make sure he was heard. Roger walked through the space where the front gate should have been and stopped about five feet behind Spence, who had done up the top two buttons on his blazer as he waited.

From within number 24 came the distant barking of a dog and then the more prominent scream of a child. *Here we go*, Roger thought, staying back, tightening his lips, a little fearful of whatever awaited them on the other side. As a footfall came towards him, Spence snapped back his neck and shoulders, puffing out his chest.

After a few seconds of low voices and movement within, the door opened and a gaunt woman half-appeared from behind it. She had long, very straight hair with a fringe that stopped halfway down her forehead. Deep lines around her mouth made her look older than she probably was. She wore bleached jeans and a matching denim jacket, tightly buttoned up.

The woman cocked back her head as a silent question.

'Mrs Molloy,' he started. 'My name is Rodney Spencer and I'm from the Antisocial Behaviour Unit of the city council.'

Spence waited for the woman to say something but she only brought a cigarette to her mouth and inhaled.

'We need to have a word,' Spence told her.

She was still thinking when another young cry came forth. Mrs Molloy turned towards the hallway.

'Ray! Tell that little cunt to fucking shut up!'

Spence glanced across at Roger.

'What is it you want?' she asked him.

'I think it's better if we chat about it indoors. Let's not give the neighbours the satisfaction, aye?'

She slowly looked him up and down and then walked into her home, leaving the front door open. Spence followed her in, Roger bringing up the rear. He put down the catch on the front door before quietly pushing it to, just as a precaution. The hall was carpeted in a worn, brown shag. Pine slats adorned the ceiling and walls. There was a smell of milk on the turn. The door that led to the kitchen was straight on and slightly ajar. Roger heard the low growl of the dog. First left off the hall was the sitting room. By the time Roger stepped up into the house, Spence was already in there.

The sitting room was unbearably hot and bore virtually no decoration. Two low three-seater settees were pushed right up to the wall. As Mrs Molloy joined the group already seated (four other women, two adolescent males), she sank deep into it, only a few inches from the ground. The air was caustic with smoke. Both young men present were dressed in the standard uniform of the ASBO recipient: prison-white running shoes, shimmering baggy track pants, American sports T-shirt and baseball cap. Each had a similarly glazed, almost cross-eyed look in their eyes. Among the cigarette women, Roger detected a physical similarity with Mrs Molloy in one or two of them. In the centre of the room stood a toddler. Roger pegged him at about eighteen months, grubby about the face, dressed only in a pull-up nappy with a large pacifier masking half his face. Spence stood, dwarfing the others, who were studiously ignoring his presence and concentrating on the room's focal point – a giant, silver-edged television, surrounded by the associated hardware of a home cinema system and a full range of Playstation paraphernalia.

They were watching CostBlast TV, a wholly owned subsidiary of PoundBlaster UK, so far up the cable channels you needed oxygen to find it. It was a shopping channel but one with a gimmick. A job lot of a particular item was put up for sale at a guide price, but the price began to fall as they began to sell. Everyone who bought the tat would get it for the price that the last person did, i.e. the lowest price, but the challenge was to either get in early and hope the price would drop sufficiently or to wait until the last minute and possibly lose out. Roger knew it well from the other visits he'd done on gaffs just like this. CostBlast TV was beaming in to giro-dependent households all over the city. Right now, a hundred-and-fifty strong lot of sculpted glass dolphins had dwindled to just five unsold. The guide price had been set at an absurd £500 but these last few were available for thirteen quid.

'*That's a saving,*' said the suited mouth on the screen, '*of £487. Can you.*' he asked, pointing straight at everyone in the room, '*afford to bypass bargains like this?*'

They all watched impassively, giving nothing away to the salesman, who kept the banter up while a list of names and places passed underneath him on the screen.

'*Only five, now only four of these beautiful items remaining. These gorgeous sculpted dolphins, or maybe they're porpoises? State your porpoise.*' he said, doing a Benny Hill salute. '*But seriously, it's just perfect for anywhere in the home. You could put them on a bookshelf or on a table. Or even as part of a dining table arrangement. Don't delay, pick up that phone like Annie from Tadcaster, Jeff from Whitley Bay, Dorothy from Rochester – she's got hers. Hi, Dorothy. Old friend of the programme. Dorothy's blasted a few prices with us over the months, isn't that right, Dorothy?*' he said, winking out from the screen.

One of the women in the room said something very fast in a strange patois that Roger couldn't make out. It made everybody else on the settees laugh out loud. Roger recognised a common exclusion tactic he'd seen on other jobs. Spence, Roger noticed, was unaffected by their efforts, so apparently engrossed was he in CostBlast TV, staring down hard at it. With only one sculpture left, the background music went up a key and quickened.

'*... down to our last one... you're going to kick yours—*'

There was a click and the sound of an explosion.

'*That's it. Twelve pounds. Another price blasted. Don't say you didn't have a chance. Our next blast is fifty sets of state-of-the-art disco lights. Don't go away...*'

Suddenly the room was quiet as the TV clicked off. Everyone looked up at Spence, who was squinting and pointing the remote control at the screen.

'That's better.' he said, putting it on the mantelpiece. 'People'll buy any old shit, aye.'

'I thought it were nice.' said one of the women.

Spence puffed out his cheeks. 'No accounting for lack of taste. OK, I'm going to be your entertainment for the next few minutes. Now then, Mrs Molloy.' he said, spinning on his heels to locate her again. 'As I said—'

'Who's this twat?' Mrs Molloy asked, pointing at Roger.

'My colleague.'

'Too scared to come by yourself?'

'That's right. He's come to hold my hand. We're here to notify you—' Spence pulled the paper out from the envelope'— that your son, Raymond... which one's Raymond?'

The two boys shared a dazed look. Silence.

'Ray-mondo?' Spence sang. 'Ah, it doesn't really matter. We're actually here to serve it on you, Mrs Molloy. If you can remember who Raymond is, you can pass on the good news.'

'Get us the cigarettes.' Mrs Molloy instructed her neighbour, a pale, blubbery blonde with red streaks in her hair and a snake tattooed on the side of her shin. Spence waved the document again.

'This is Raymond's very own Antisocial Behaviour Order. With this document, the council is serving notice on you that your son must constrain his future behaviour.'

The comedienne among them made another unintelligible aside, causing much dark amusement, although Mrs Molloy didn't smile that much. Spence was undeterred and began to recite from the order. Roger sensed with some concern that he was savouring the theatre of the situation. With the two lads obviously coming up fast on their pills, Roger sensed an atmosphere that lay on the cusp between lazy contempt and sudden aggression.

'That means that he must not—'

'I need a fucking fag. This cunt's doing my nerves in.'

'—use foul or abusive language or threatening language towards any other person—'

Mrs Molloy grabbed the pack of Embassy Regal when they were offered and lit one up, hands trembling.

'He may not use racist or homophobic language or behaviour to any resident or member of the public—'

Mrs Molloy looked towards the window and the world outside it. The toddler stepped across and tried to grab the fags from her hand.

'—what else we got here?' said Spence, turning the page. 'Oh yeah. He may not enter the PoundBlaster Handy Convenience Store on Meades Road or harass members of staff working at that store.'

Another garbled comment and another laugh, the boy who was probably Raymond shuffling on the settee and grinning lopsidedly.

'He may not enter the Alabammy Fried Chicken Restaurant, also on Meades Road.'

General hilarity now, even Mrs Molloy cackling dryly.

'Glad you're all enjoying this... He may not intentionally damage or attempt to damage property or possessions not belonging to him or council buildings and facilities...' Spence scanned down the letter. 'Where's the bit about curfew? Here we go... In order to limit the possibility of further antisocial behaviour, Raymond is also required to remain here at this address during the hours of nine in the evening to seven the following morning every day...'

'Eh?' Mrs Molloy asked. The one who must have been Raymond sat forward, head lolling. 'Wowozzat, mate?' he asked.

But Spence wasn't being distracted.

'If you wish to seek to amend these terms for special circumstances.' he rattled on, 'you will have to seek a variation in this order. You got that?... There's just one other thing...'

'Everything getting blamed on my Ray.' muttered Mrs Molloy, her attention partly distracted by the reluctance of her next cigarette to come out of the packet. 'He gets fucking blamed for everything.'

'... Er, OK. Raymond is banned from being part of a group of more than three people in a public place whose presence and behaviour there is likely to cause harassment, alarm and distress...'

Mrs Molloy got up and picked up the small child. Spence took a step back towards the door.

'By the way, Raymond? Do you know someone called Curtis Barclay?'

Again, looks exchanged but no reply.

'It says here you do. Anyway, the point being that, from this moment forward, you are forbidden from seeing him, speaking to him on the phone or in any way associating with him' Spence gave him a sad smile. 'Not even a Christmas card.'

This was too much for Mrs Molloy, who took a sharp breath and charged him.

'Right, that's it! You're dead! Shane!'

Roger made straight for the front door, hearing Spence behind him, rattling off the stuff about how a breach of the conditions could lead to a fine or a custodial sentence. Back outside, Roger felt the cold air stinging his eye again, making it water. He was near the end of the path when Spence came tripping down the steps outside the front door, almost laughing as Mrs Molloy swung a kick at him, the baby hauled up under her armpit.

'You fucking come here, me with my nerves the way they are, you fucking…I'll have your fucking job…'

'You want to calm down, love.' said Spence. 'Take a powder.'

Mrs Molloy stepped back, expertly spinning and lowering the child before disappearing behind the front door. When she emerged again, it was with a two-litre bottle of PoundBlaster bleach in both hands. The top was off. Swinging it low, she launched a long, wide streak of liquid right at Spence, who swayed aside at the last possible moment with the experience of someone who'd dodged more perilous attacks. Behind him, Roger stood still, watching the bleach on its parabola down in front of him. He was disappointed to see that, after splashing on the mottled concrete of the Molloys' path, a small amount had bounced forward and on to the tips of his shoes. He looked up at Mrs Molloy, who was bent forward but drawing the bottle back, preparing to give it another go. She stopped briefly, noticing something.

'You crying?' she asked, almost outraged.

Spence slipped the ASBO back into the envelope and flung it, frisbee like, at Mrs Molloy's feet. He then turned and leaped the garden wall, unable to keep the smile off his face. This additional taunt was lost on Mary Molloy, who had her attention fixed on Roger.

'Oi, you seen this? Are you crying? This cunt's fucking crying.'

'It's conjunctivitis.' he said, stepping backwards quickly, back into the street, keeping his itchy, weeping eye on Mrs Molloy as the PoundBlaster bleach bottle reached the end of its backswing. 'It's conjunctivitis, you stupid, ugly, evil bitch.'

Her next bleach attack was less potent. It missed him easily.

'You don't come to my house and call me ugly!' proclaimed

Mrs Molloy. 'Just for that, I'm going to have your fucking job. Shane!' she summoned, hollering deep into the house. 'Shane! Come out and chin this cunt and his cunt boyfriend!'

Roger heard a noise of movement from where he assumed the kitchen must have been. Mrs Molloy was becoming emotional. Spence was continuing his walk back to the car but Roger stopped for a moment, just to watch.

'You come to my own house.' Mrs Molloy was saying, the tears welling up. 'With my nerves the way they are, you come to my house. My Ray's always…it's not fair…'

Roger looked on, impassive, as still holding the door she slid down on to the doorstep, her legs folding underneath her as she succumbed to a sobbing fit. This was not uncommon but it fascinated him none the less, the acting out of some primordial psychological one-way system. He knew that this, the lachrymose victim spell, the nervous breakdown in miniature, probably acted out at least half a dozen times a day, would be followed by a new offensive, more random, more apocalyptic in scale. As usual in such matters, he was right. With a low moan, Mrs Molloy dragged herself half upwards until she was bent double, clutching her stomach with one hand, jabbing her cigarette repeatedly towards him.

'My nerves…I could fucking die. You're just going to leave me dying here. I'll tell you this, you dirty bastard. I'll tell you something. If I die 'cause of you, when I'm dead I'll fucking come back to haunt you. I'll come back and I'll kill you all in your sleep. I'll kill your kids and your mother and your cunt father!'

Roger sniffed.

'You're too late.' he hollered, surprised at the sound of his own voice. 'He died last night.'

Mrs Molloy drew herself erect once more, gently sucking on her Embassy filter as if somehow seeing justice done.

'Good.' she said. 'That's made my day. He was just the

first. I'll come in your sleep and cut your fucking throat. SHANE!'

Spence was standing on the passenger's side, waiting for the car to be unlocked. Resisting the urge to break into a trot, Roger returned to his vehicle with a measured step, aware of activity behind him. Opening the central locking with his electronic key, they both got in and he slid quickly behind the wheel, looking up just as he started the ignition. He saw a man he didn't recognise, early forties, topless, in another pair of shimmering track pants, coming towards the car. A complicated sequence of multicoloured tattoos across chest and shoulders were sympathetically displayed on his sinewy body by the angle at which he held an aluminium baseball bat above his head. Spence might have expected a cry of intent to be coming from his mouth, but the man was silent, concentrated. He'd done this kind of thing before.

Roger snapped the car into reverse and hit the accelerator hard. With a backward squeal of his tyres, he pulled away enough to spin the car a hundred and eighty degrees and still be ahead of the attacker. But it was a close thing. The tattooed man had built up enough momentum to stay in touch, although still too far away to get the swing in at a windshield he was obviously after. Finding first gear and suddenly feeling the road grip beneath him and the car accelerate away, Roger could see the reds of his eyes in his rear-view mirror as he drew his upper body back and up and launched the bat roughly towards them. It flew like a tomahawk, scything the air, landing just short of the car, but rearing up violently on contact with the road, smacking the back window.

'Stop!' insisted Spence.

Instinctively, Roger hit the brakes.

'What?' Roger asked but Spence had already opened his door.

'Just a sec.'

He got out. Roger was faintly aware of footsteps, more than one set he was sure, slapping in their direction at speed. In his wing mirror he could see Spence move down the side of the car. There, just behind it, was the bat, its progress having continued until it lay only a few feet away. Spence bent down and picked it up before returning to the car, holding it in both hands. Getting back inside, he threw it on the back seat and smiled at Roger.

'Souvenir.' he said.

Roger sat with the engine running, hand on the gear stick. He could see them coming in the mirror, four of them running hard. He knew Spence was looking at him, wondering what he was doing, but there was a part of Roger, a newer part, that wanted to take things to the absolute last moment, to see how close he could get to disaster and avoid it. He dreaded violence to his own person, but it was negligent not to see how close you could get.

He wanted *involvement*.

He sped away at what he hoped was the absolute last moment, alarmed yet excited at the fist smacking the back window. As he hit a pothole, the baseball bat bounced behind him with a clang, as if it had a will of its own.

Spence sat twisted in the passenger seat for the next thirty seconds, watching the scene behind them dwindle until Roger took a left turn and it disappeared altogether. Spence threw himself round and forward, not bothering with the seatbelt.

'That.' he announced, 'was a crack. Have to do that again some time. Absolute nutters.' he sniggered.

'You could have got us both killed.'

'Christ, they were just toying with us. That was nothing. These lads at the unit, they do that every day.' Spence didn't spend a lot of time at the unit. He generally had other fish to fry.

'Most days.'

'No wonder they're all mad bastards.'

'Maybe they don't provoke them like that.'

'Provoke? What did I do to provoke them?'

'You turned off the shopping channel, for Christ's sake! That's like bombing Pearl Harbor. You got a death wish or something?'

Spence laughed. '—Seriously, man, I'll tell you what. Some stranger walks into my house and tells one of my family what they can and can't do, I'd feel bloody provoked.'

'You can be a bit more diplomatic.'

Spence scoffed.

'Diplomatic? Did you hear what I was reading in there? Have you ever heard anything so fucking—' he thought about it, choosing the right word '—illiberal?'

Roger shook his head.

'They're all like that. That's what an ASBO is. It's an order. You break it, you pay the consequences.'

Spence made a show of surprise.

'Listen to you. What about innocent until proven guilty? What about a fair trial? What about—' he waved his hand, struggling for a fitting finale '—the Magna Carta?'

Roger laughed.

'I'm serious, man. Some of that stuff... Fucking... that bit where it said he couldn't be seen with that... who was it?'

'Curtis Barclay. He's known. Their pusher, most likely.'

'Doesn't matter. Doesn't matter if he's Carlos the Jackal. Saying he can't hang around with who he wants... that's a human right, isn't it? Freedom of... whatnot?'

'Freedom of Assembly and Association. Article Eleven.'

Spence did his well-rehearsed double-take.

'How do you know that?'

Roger smirked and tapped himself on the chest. 'You forget, Mr Bond. Human Rights Act Liaison Unit, 2000 to 2002.'

Spence threw back his head and laughed, a different point

proven. 'Don't get me wrong. I couldn't give a shit about Ratboy back there and his chav family. It just needs to be pointed out. You can't say boo to a goose to anybody else, but when it comes to the charvie scum it's OK to come down like a ton of bricks.'

'They make people's lives a misery.'

'Of course they do. But look, man. You plant a bomb in a shopping centre and you end up with more rights than these people. The thing about this lot.' said Spence, gesturing back at the Gildenhall, 'is that nobody, and I mean nobody, gives a shit about them. Christ, gypsies get treated better. Bloody pikeys have got the treehuggers throwing themselves at their feet. Nobody goes into bat for the white trash. Imagine the council ordering a gyppo not to walk into a kebab shop. There'd be uproar. Uproar.'

Roger couldn't help but be amused by Spence's tirade. 'You're the great entrepreneur. Distribute some of that wealth. You help them.'

Spence shook his head.

'That might be taking principle too far. Anyway, business not so good at the mo.'

Despite his self-imposed sanction on knowing the detail of Spence's business dealings, Roger's curiosity got the better of him. 'No?' he enquired.

Spence made a face. 'Peter bloody Pease.'

Roger raised an eyebrow. Councillor Pease was the recently elected city supremo for resources with responsibility for budgetary restraint after the council had had its funding from central government capped. Having marked out his territory by announcing a complete investigation of the council's expenses payments, it was clear there was no cupboard he wasn't prepared to rattle the skeletons in. His enthusiastic tightening of the council's purse strings was obviously already hindering Spence's money-making opportunities.

'Hard case, is he?'

Spence huffed. 'Seen it all before. Spends all his time glopping off over his spreadsheets, whatever they are. He'll get tired of scrabbling around for fifty ps and move on. Maniac like him, he has to be after a parliamentary seat.'

Roger shook his head.

'He's an independent, isn't he?'

Spence looked worried.

'What's that mean?'

'Means that he doesn't have a party. Doesn't have any political ambition.'

This didn't compute with Spence.

'So what's he there for?'

Roger took his hand off the wheel to give an approximation of a salute. 'Public service.'

Spence closed his eyes and began rubbing the ridge of his nose. 'Public service? Fuck me! Is nothing sacred?' he moaned.

2

It was very hot in Mrs Dawkin's office and Roger's nose had stuffed up. He was aware that, being forced to breathe through his mouth, his throat was getting dry. Besides the temperature, Roger felt generally uncomfortable. When Mrs Dawkin had telephoned him to tell him that his father had been discovered that morning in a deceased state, Roger had resolved to dress smartly before arriving to meet her, considerably smarter than he would for work. Having dropped Spence off at a pub he had an unofficial share in, Roger had put on a tie, but that had meant doing up the top button on his shirt, which had started to nip his neck. His unfamiliarity with wearing a tie was also causing a reaction. It had the effect of tightening up his left shoulder, which he had to keep lifting and rolling backwards for relief, cocking his head to one side at the same time. Every time he did it, he could hear the clicking of the joint, the cracking of his bones as they wrestled themselves back into position. After every twitch, the discomfort would come back, slightly more intense. He was forced to twitch again, then twist his neck violently. The tension simply increased until he sat there, fantasising about having his arm ripped out from its socket, the only final means of relief possible.

'Are you all right, Mr Merrion?' asked Mrs Dawkin, who had just returned to her desk facing him after an expedition to her filing cabinet for his father's details.

'Bit tense.' he explained, twitching and twisting and taking the opportunity to massage his shoulder blade with his right hand.

'Well, that's understandable.' said Mrs Dawkin with a thin smile. She was a big woman, top-heavy with androgyny, heavily lipsticked, with a mass of unruly thick hair. Roger thought he detected the trace of an Afrikaans accent. As she talked about arrangements following the unfortunate loss of his father, flicking through the file in front of her, Roger wondered how many old people she had killed. It wasn't a question of whether she had ever done the smothering or the slow poisoning, it was simply a question of numbers. A handful, dozens, hundreds?

'We can make the funeral arrangements, if you prefer.' she said.

Despite his efforts at self-relief, the ache in his shoulder was becoming more chronic. He had no recourse but to shoot his left arm up in the air and pull it downwards behind his head in an approximation of a yoga position he'd seen on television in the small hours during one of his recent attacks of insomnia.

'Yes, that would be fine.' he told her.

'Mr Merrion, would you like some medical assistance?'

Roger eyed her suspiciously. A consultation, a few words of comfort and a hypodermic in the arm, was that it? Her Munchausen's by proxy was clearly habitual now; she rolled the suggestion off with something like boredom. But it wasn't an entirely unattractive proposition for Roger. He slept so badly these days that a long rest, a *permanent* rest, had some appeal.

'No.' he said. 'I'll be fine.'

'Perhaps an osteopath…'

'Yes.' Maybe Mrs Dawkin would offer to click him around herself, don a white coat she had on the back of the door and then dutifully break his neck for him. The possibility of death hung off her like a druid's robe.

She readdressed the file. 'There is the matter of your father's effects. We'd be grateful if they could be removed as soon as possible. All those books, they do rather collect dust…'

Mrs Dawkin's displeasure at her father's library was no secret. She had raised objections when he had moved in with them, but Dad had been adamant. His leather-bound collected works of Marx were, ironically enough, the only possession he really clung on to with any vestige of bourgeois pride. Whether his dad had ever read them or not, Roger didn't really know. It wasn't important. The discomfort they gave Mrs Dawkin and her ilk was their true function, especially after his father had been forbidden from upsetting the other residents by talking politics during bingo.

'I'll take them now, if you have some boxes.'

Mrs Dawkin looked up and stared at him.

'Boxes. Of course. That would be most generous. The rest of his effects?…We have an arrangement regarding clothes with a local charity.'

Roger nodded, wondering what her cut would be from the sale of his father's collection of three-piece suits.

Roger sat in the room that had for a short time been his father's. The bed had already been stripped and the curtains removed. Soulless and dark, like a thousand rooms on the Gildenhall and every other estate across town.

He caught a view of himself in the mirror. Medium height, lightish hair cut short, thin nose, full mouth. Same as yesterday. He peered forward to look closer. His right eye looked redder than the other one. He blinked twice and then, as if on cue, felt the itchiness around his tear duct again. Conjunctivitis coming back. Teasing the flesh around his eye back, he sat down again. There was a box at his feet, empty. Facing him were the books his father had left behind, the socialist gospels by which he had led his life. In this spirit, Dad liked the fact that Roger worked for the local council and took his work far more seriously than Roger himself ever had. He hadn't been sure about Roger's latest job, though.

'Nuisance neighbours, did you say?'

'Sort of.'

Dad had nodded firmly. He was a great believer in something called social fabric, which he purported to understand as a concept.

'No.' he'd said. 'Socialist thinking is quite firm on this point. Standards of public behaviour were invented by the bloody working class. What happens to these people?'

Roger had shrugged.

'They get a verbal warning, then a written warning. Then, if it carries on, they could get evicted.'

Dad had gone quiet on hearing this. In asking the question, he had anticipated a Utopian response. Uncomfortable reality had a habit of doing this to him. His inherent love of the underdog regularly put him in this kind of quandary.

'Of course, it's not entirely their fault. They've been brought up with no political conscience. They don't know any better. They really get evicted?'

As Roger had hoped, the old man had gone out without any pain over and above the average. Although it was difficult to tell with his dad, who loathed being set apart, as if this somehow compromised his commitment to the brotherhood of man. *It's the same for everybody,* Dad would often say. *Why should I be treated any differently?*

Roger began to pull the rest of the books off the shelves

and pack them neatly into the boxes. Once that had been done, he collected up the small objects: reading glasses, cuff-links, the fountain pen and bottle of ink. And the anglepoise lamp on his desk had been Dad's own, a superior model to the chatty one provided by the home which now sat in a drawer, strangled by its own cord. The task completed, he thought there surely must be something more for him to do. But everything seemed to have been taken care of.

Roger got into his car and drove. His time at Dad's final address had been shorter than he expected. A lot shorter. It was still just about light. He didn't want to go home when it was still light. He wanted time alone, so he drove, finding himself on the dual carriageway that meandered through the old heart of the city, dipping and rising like a tired rollercoaster before reluctantly straightening up and heading north. As he passed underneath them, the blue motorway signs gave him a momentary sense of possibility. If he held the course he was on, he'd soon find himself with three lanes of fast road ahead, destination unknown. Destination irrelevant. He remembered the song;

> *Got a wife and kids in Baltimore, Jack*
> *I went out for a ride and I never went back...*

He came off at the last possible junction and headed back to the city.

3

As he pushed open the front door, Roger could sense the effort that had been put in for his return home. The house was tidy most of the time but Marion had really been over the place this time. The lights were on throughout the house, making it look warm against the gloom of the evening. There were fresh flowers in the hallway.

He let the front door slam behind him to announce his presence. With unnatural haste, the handle on one of the connecting doors snapped down and Marion emerged from the kitchen, wearing an apron. Dark casserole smells overtook her as she came out to meet him, stopping a couple of paces from him as he took off his coat.

'Well?' she asked, gently.

'Yeah.' Roger replied, pushing his lips tightly together. 'Everything's in hand.'

He took a step past her but she stopped him, a hand on his wrist, and reached up to kiss him on the cheek. He turned and reached down to embrace her before they both walked through into the kitchen. She followed him. He sat down at the table. She went back to hovering around the stove.

'I'd like to hear about it. It'll probably help you as well, to talk about it.'

Roger shrugged.

'There isn't much to tell. I went there this morning and they said he went during the night. They suggested I come back later, so I went to work. Then I went back and packed away some of his stuff and that was it. They'll call tomorrow about the funeral arrangements.'

'Cremation, you think?' she asked.

Roger widened his eyes. Marion often liked to converse in a self-consciously grown-up way, like the characters did in the novels she read. Death was one of the subjects that lent itself to this type of deep discourse. Roger probably preferred Spence's more irreverent tone. After all, what was happening to him happened to everyone at one time or another. He didn't like the idea of playing it for all it was worth.

God, thought Roger. *I sound just like him. I'm turning into my old man.*

'Roger?' Marion interrupted the thought.

'Sorry?'

'Cremation was what he wanted, wasn't it?'

'Suppose.'

She waited a moment.

'So, what else happened? I mean, did you actually see him?'

Roger considered the question. The way she'd asked it suggested some doubt in her mind. Dad could be a contrary bastard, but Roger doubted he would fake his own end. Besides, when Mrs Dawkin said you were dead, it had the ring of truth.

'No. He was gone... He'd been taken by the time I got there. They'd emptied his room by this afternoon.'

'Really?' Marion said with a shiver. 'It seems so cold.'

Roger found himself shrugging again.

'That's the business they're in.'

She sighed. 'I suppose you're right. It's just... the reality of it, someone being there one minute and then not the next...'

Stepping back, she undid her apron, revealing what Roger suspected was a new outfit. A black shirt, drawn in at the hips, was tucked into a pair of jeans, which hugged her thighs. As she sat down at the table next to him, he realised that she'd had her hair done. Probably. He wondered what signals he was supposed to be picking up from all this. He couldn't get away from the notion that she was treating it like a special occasion.

Reaching forward, she placed a hand on his knee. Roger detected a hint of cleavage through the gaps in her shirt buttons. He felt an urge to reach out and seize her breasts, seize them with a degree of controlled violence even, but he resisted. He didn't want to upset her when she had gone to all this effort.

'I just wanted to say.' she said quietly, beginning a rehearsed speech, 'that I want you to know we're all here for you. Just remember, even though Brian's gone, you still have family. We're your family. And we love you.'

Roger took her hand and squeezed it. The use of his father's Christian name had jarred; it took him a second to work out who she was talking about. He considered a response but decided that it was better to say nothing. She brought her other hand into play, rubbing across his knuckles with her thumb.

'I told the kids to give us a few minutes.' she explained, answering a question that didn't exist. 'I just wanted a moment with you to myself. Because there was something else I wanted to...' She looked down. 'If you wanted to come back into my bed, then—' she looked up again and straight into his eyes '—that would be OK...'

Roger nodded and smiled. *A fresh start?* he wondered. He met her halfway as she leaned in for a kiss. Their lips met and held for a long beat. When they parted, she rose quickly and opened the door that led through to the living room, a signal for the kids that their tête-à-tête was over.

'Can you get me a drink?' she asked cheerily, her volume distinctly higher. 'I bought a nice bottle.'

Roger got up and idly went to pick up a copy of the *Argus* lying on the worktop. Marion, however, snatched it from him and dispatched it quickly in the bin by her feet. 'Don't.' she said. 'Too depressing. That disgusting Bronsky man. The things he's supposed to have done to those children, I can't see why they have to print them in such detail.' She shivered at the memory. 'I know it's wrong in most cases but there are some people they should have capital punishment for. I'd press the button myself to see that pig swing. Anyway, how was work?'

'Yeah, all right.' said Roger, struggling with the smartarse corkscrew he'd been bought for Christmas and didn't really know how to use. 'I did a job with Spence. He pulled his usual and it all got a bit hairy.'

She clicked her tongue. 'Typical.'

Before she'd packed it in to give birth to Beth, Marion had worked for the council. It was how they had met. She liked to engage in conversations about it, using terminology and acronyms that had long since fallen into disuse. Roger never tried to correct her, thinking it a bit infra dig when she had packed it in from a sense of duty to her notion of family and not because she wanted to. She remembered Spence from the old days.

'You want to be careful around him.' she commented, starting to lay the table.

'Careful of who?'

This was Nick, standing in the doorway in his Metallica T-shirt, rubbing his eyes. Remembering Spence's comment, Roger watched his son a little more carefully than normal.

'Can you do this?' Roger asked him, holding up the corkscrew, the bottle dangling unnaturally beneath it. Nick took it from him.

'How you feeling?' he asked Roger, setting about the cork. 'You're all right with it? Grandad and everything?'

'Yeah. I'm all right with it.'

The cork came out.

'I'm up for coming to the funeral and everything, you know.' said Nick, handing over the bottle with a yawn.

'Tired?' Roger asked, a trace of admonishment in his voice.

'Playstation.' came the reply. 'Doing my head in.'

Marion clicked her tongue.

'You bought it for me, remember?' Nick pointed out.

'Beginning to regret it.' said Marion, putting out some rarely sighted linen napkins.

'Anyway.' Nick wanted to know, 'who've you got to be careful of?'

'A man your father works with.'

'You ever heard me talk about Spence?'

Nick couldn't remember.

'He's just a grandstander, that's all. We had to go and serve an ASBO on a family on the Gildenhall and they took umbrage. One of them tried throwing a bottle of bleach over us.'

Nick's bleary eyes widened.

'Aw-right. Dad mixing it with the white trash. Like it.'

Marion wasn't impressed. 'I can't believe you have to have anything to do with those people.'

'They're just people.' ventured Nick, peering into the casserole dish. 'They're not, like, murderers or something. They're just not enfranchised like you are. So they do what they want.'

'How come you know so much about them?'

Nick cocked his head. 'Er, 'cause maybe you sent me to school with hundreds of them. Not that many of them turn up after year nine, mind.'

'What do you mean? If you didn't go to school, your father and me, we'd be sent to prison.'

Nick smacked her a quick kiss on the cheek.

'Mum, you're a great cook but there's a load of shit going on out there you don't know anything about. It's us and them. And there's more and more of them and you can't change them. One day they'll win and we'll all be like them. Live with it.'

Marion shook her head. 'You have to believe people can change for the better.'

Nick shrugged, in a way that reminded Roger of himself.

'Yeah, but why should they? What's in it for them? Nobody gives a toss about them, so why shouldn't they have some fun?'

'So you think it's OK to behave like that?' asked his mother.

'I'm not saying it's right. Or wrong. I'll leave the judging to others. I'm just saying that's what they think. Can I have a glass of wine?'

'Sure.' said Roger before Marion could say no.

'You might want to water it down.' she suggested.

'Whatever.' Nick said.

'Dinner's nearly ready.' Marion pointed out. 'Go and get your sister.'

When Beth rushed into the kitchen, a couple of minutes later, she threw both arms around Roger and hugged him hard.

'Oh, Dad. I'm so sorry. I wanted to see you as soon as you were here but I'm just lost in my own world with all this history revision...'

Nick sniggered as he dragged a chair from under the table and sat on it. Beth rose to the bait.

'Piss off, Nicholas. Just wait 'til you've got mocks to worry about.'

'Hmm.' said Nick. 'Can't see how talking all goo-goo on

the phone to Marcus Carr is going to help you remember Hitler's war aims. Plus the fact he's only one rung up the ladder from your chavs on the Gildenhall.'

Beth didn't quite get what he meant but she knew she didn't like it.

'Sod off, Nicholas. You're such a kid.'

'Whereas you, of course, are so adult it hurts...'

'Cut it out.' snapped Marion. 'The two of you. Tonight of all nights, can we not just have a civilised mealtime?'

Roger sat down at the table with a strange sense of disappointment. Something about the bickering of his children, their ability to know just what buttons to push, entertained him. They didn't mean anything by it. And besides, it felt *normal*, set against the artificiality of Marion's stage-management.

The casserole was good. Roger ate hurriedly, aware of an expectation that he should be talking about Dad and ashamed that he had nothing to say.

His plate empty, he refilled his glass and stood up, sensing Marion's disappointment. She had obviously envisaged some quality time around the table as part of her perfect evening.

'That was delicious.' he told her. 'Beth, love, go back to your revision if you like. And as for you.' he said, grabbing Nick in a gentle headlock, 'you're going to show me how to beat you at Playstation.'

Half an hour of *War on Terror II: Wind of Revenge* later and Roger was in pain. His eyes stung and his shoulders, neck and back ached from sitting cross-legged on the floor while he'd been graphically killed about a dozen times. To soften the blows of repeated and violent death, he'd drunk most of the wine single-handed and could feel a dry, tannic rime across the back of his teeth. When Marion had passed through, she looked a little disappointed when the announcement that she was going upstairs was met with a wave of the hand and a whoop of murderous joy at the maiming of a hooded jihadist.

'Eat lead, raghead!' Nick had cried, making his dad laugh.

When they finally switched it off, with Nick wanting to watch a movie on one of the cable channels, Roger felt tired but restless, didn't much fancy lying on the single bed in the loft extension, staring up at the ceiling for hours on end. As Roger stretched his back, Nick backed himself up on to the settee, suddenly looking puzzled and digging a hand under the cushions.

'Bollocks!'

'What's the matter?' asked Roger.

Nick held up a plastic video box.

'Shit. This was supposed to go back tonight.'

Roger sniffed. 'I'll take it.'

'Yeah? You sure?'

'I could do with the fresh air.'

Nick flung it across. Roger caught it.

By the time he reached the video store, it had closed. He put the box into the night return slot and decided to take a different, extended route home through the streets where he'd lived all his life.

Roger walked a long way, shoulders hunched, hands shoved deep into coat pockets. He had hoped that this day, when it came, would complete what felt like the process of his life up to this point. It would be an end and a beginning. A new stage of life sounded good, but why was there no discernible sensation to go with it? Why didn't he feel anything?

Truth was, he was up for a spot of catharsis.

He found that he had stopped walking. He was staring at a piece of paper someone had attached to a lamppost with Sellotape.

LOST KITTEN, it read. He scanned the text. A crudely

photocopied image of the animal lay beneath the words. In the low glow, little Fluff stared up dolefully, right at Roger. Looking at it for a few seconds, he burst uncontrollably into tears.

He walked for some time, having to stop whenever the sobbing overtook him again. Then he gave himself time to recover before heading for home with a quiet determination. Unsure how long he'd been away, he found himself back at his own front door. All the lights were off. Letting himself back in quietly, he collected a family bag of crisps and a two-litre bottle of PoundBlaster Coke from the kitchen, picking up his wallet where he had left it on the bench and grabbing the phone from its recharger before heading back through to the lounge. With the bottle of pop and the crisps nestled beside him, he began clicking up the cable channels until he found what he was looking for.

He watched for a few minutes before pulling out his credit card. Then he picked up the phone, dialled the number on the screen and, in a dream-like state, made his first-ever purchase from CostBlast TV.

4

Roger was back at the driver's wheel of his car, seat reclined, deep in mid-afternoon ennui. Heath Mason was positioned at a forty-five-degree angle towards him in the passenger seat.

From where Roger had parked, they were well placed to watch what was going on outside the magistrates' court on the opposite side of the busy road. A small crowd had gathered under a warm sky, maybe thirty or forty people positioned halfway between the canopied entrance and the gated side road where police and security vehicles entered and departed from the site.

Mason had been watching the constituent members of the crowd through his mini-binoculars for a while, citing the odd name of someone he recognised.

'Sandra McGinty there... Tyler Ward. Tyler, Tyler, Tyler, what are you doing here...?'

The usual suspects, Roger inferred, taking the penultimate bite from his very late lunch of a bagel and washing it down with a glug from a warm can of Red Blast. He burped.

'Phoaar.' said Mason, waving his hand in front of his face. 'That stuff stinks.'

Roger inspected the can. 'Tastes fucking awful too, as it

happens.'

'What you drinking it for?'

'Stay awake. Can't seem to sleep at night.' he said quietly, recalling his CostBlast frenzy the previous night. Seeing his name flashing across the bottom of the screen ('*Hi there, Roger, good to have you along...*'), he'd been thrilled by an overwhelming sense of inclusion. Thinking he'd finally found the solution to his chronic insomnia, he'd rarely known such disappointment than to discover the channel closed down at 2 a.m.

Mason sighed. 'Come on.' he muttered, picking up the field glasses again. 'Let's have some action.'

Like most of the young guns on the ASBU, Mason was always looking for action. Unlike Roger and Spence, Mason had joined the unit in the expectation of it, in the hope of a regular rumble with the chav classes. Unaffected by the kind of doubts that Spence had been voicing the day before, the young guns were distributors of justice and liked to dress up, often sporting black raincoats and sunglasses, like in *The Matrix*, to serve ASBOs on the enemy. Mason had an unnatural interest in his work but at least that meant he was prepared to do more than his share. Even now, when they were nominally on their delayed meal break, he was scanning the crowd outside the court for antisoc celebrity. Putting the bins back up to his face, though, he chose to focus in on an advertising hoarding away to their right. The poster he was studying, on such a scale as to make the binoculars redundant, was for a brand of clothing. The image was of a teenage girl in a rainbow-coloured vest and bikini bottoms held together on her hips by two lengths of string, lying on her side, head propped on one hand. She had long dark hair and distinctive Latin features. She had looked straight at the camera and now straight out at the world, her lips parted slightly, about to make thrilling promises.

'How old can she be?' Mason asked, squinting behind the

eyepieces. 'How old do you reckon? Thirteen? Twelve?'

Roger let out a breath.

'No, but it's weird.' Mason speculated. 'There's this weird kind of...' he struggled with his own idea. 'It's, like, the more that they say something is wrong, like having sex with...' He pointed at the poster. 'Underage. The more we say it's taboo, the more people are talking about it... the more people start thinking about it *as a possibility*. Maybe that nonce in there—' he gestured over to the courts '—maybe he wouldn't even have thought of it until someone came on the telly and told him that he was already thinking of shagging little boys. You know what I mean?'

Roger swayed his head from side to side. Mason was always keen you knew what he meant. That was understandable. Misinterpretation was a constant danger in the council milieu and accounted, at least in part, for the chronic incoherence in its halls of power. Misinterpretation could lead to suspension, dismissal or, more likely, your instant categorisation into one of the many untouchable clans: racist, sexist, homophobic and, perhaps worst of all, *determinist*. The best policy, Roger had learned long ago, was to say little in certain company and, when you did, make sure it was free of all opinion. There was a look he had mastered. The council stare, he thought of it as. A tightening of the mouth and a widening of the eyes, perhaps a little shrug. It could be interpreted as anything but pinned down as nothing.

Anticipating a long wait, he turned on the radio, which was tuned to Civic, the local commercial station. They listened to an ad for PoundBlaster's monthly specials in reverential silence before the programming returned. It was nearing the end of the afternoon phone-in, hosted, as it had been for many years, by Johnny Odom, that great ambassador for the city and the wonderful people in and of it. His strange, boozed-up features, complete with sunglasses and ponytail, stared out from the backs of buses all over town, arranged in a troubling smile.

Roger never listened to Odom's show almost as a matter of principle but something about today, with his mind still on his father, made it seem appropriate. For Odom was a man who shared a common past with Roger's dad. In a previous incarnation, as the suited and booted J.P. Odom in the late 1960s and right though the 1970s, he had led the municipal authority's Planning and Construction Department in a glut of destruction and redevelopment that had changed the face of the city. Whatever it had truly been like before (always a subject of debate and dispute), he was the man who'd taken the concrete scalpel to it and made it the hard-faced bitch it was today. The meaningless flyovers and underpasses that littered the place were testament to the working of Odom's mind. 'The future.' he once famously stated at a civic function attended by the Prime Minister, 'has come to me as if in a dream. I am not a selfish man. In the true spirit of socialism, I will share and redistribute the dream.' Two weeks later, with his OBE in the bag and the wrecking balls swinging across the city, he was arrested on charges of corruption after receiving significant bribes to promote an industrialised housing system invented in Czechoslovakia called Skurj. He got seven years and served three. While he languished behind bars, gaining a much-publicised degree in Renaissance Studies from the Open University, the city of his dreams went up around him. On his release, with half the population expecting him to be lynched by the other half, he was put under police protection until he was able, in his own words, to 'win back the hearts of the people through the medium of hospital radio'. Then on to the Civic phone-in, where his lifelong fight for his fellow citizens found new impetus.

The current caller was taking issue with a notification he'd received to stop playing his record collection at unacceptable volumes. Johnny, as ever, had an opinion.

'Listen, my friend, noise pollution is a serious problem for lots of people. I mean, I'm thinking you're not living on a forty-acre estate, am I right?'

'No. I live in rented accommodation.'

'A flat?'

'A flat. But Johnny, an Englishman's home is his castle. I need to play it loud. It helps me to chill and I'm a recovering alcoholic and I need... to... chill. You with me?'

Johnny grunted in what might have been sympathy. 'I hear you, my friend. But, I mean, I can't condone that if it's upsetting your neighbours.'

'Yeah, but the bag next door reckons she's deaf. If she's deaf, how can she complain about it?'

The logic was too much for Odom, who cut him off.

'Next caller?'

Mason pointed to some movement outside the court.

'Aye, aye.' he said, back on the binoculars. 'Here we go.'

With relief, Roger turned the radio off. The two large metal gates slowly opened and a dozen or so coppers stepped out to line the road. Shortly afterwards, two police vans emerged at fair speed. The crowd, having already surged forward at the first sign of action, splintered, as some individuals tried to pass the thin police line. Objects were flung at the second of the two vehicles, a sequence of small windows high up along its side. What looked like large house-brick fragments bounced off it and a streak of red liquid, probably paint, attached itself about halfway up.

'Ha!' Mason cried. 'That was Charlene Duffy. I think that constitutes a breach of your ASBO, Charlene, don't you, love?' He suddenly sat bolt upright. 'Oh…aha, I love it. That's Barry Cox, the one who just flung the bottle. I only served on him last week. He's not allowed to cough unless we say so.'

Roger smiled, more in wonder at Mason's astonishing

knowledge of his subject than the antics out front. A few of the crowd, middle-aged women mostly, had managed to get out and were rushing the van. One of them had come from nowhere to throw herself on the road in front of the lead vehicle, which was forced to stop.

Mason started taking notes, and Roger looked on as the cadre of vigilantes began hammering on the sides of the van, screaming abuse. The police struggled to remove the prone protester blocking the way. As soon as she was lifted out, someone else took her place.

A couple of young men, recognised immediately by Mason despite the baseball caps pulled down over their faces, were grappling with the handles on the rear doors of the van. With the way cleared, they clung on to the back door as the van began to move again, hammering on the darkened glass.

The two boys were prised from the van and it sped away, braking hard at the next junction and squealing a sharp turn away.

'Got enough?' Roger asked Mason, who nodded hard, still transferring what he'd witnessed on to the pages of his pad.

'Plenty. Five breaches, I reckon. Five little townies caught right in the act.'

The mood in the crowd, its point made, changed to one of high spirits. Inside the van, Victor Bronsky, the alleged paedophile making his first pre-trial appearance at the magistrates' court, would have got the message.

5

Back at the office, Roger was surprised to see Spence there, telling the others about Mary Molloy with his usual penchant for the Gothic.

'You should have heard her. She was great. She put a fucking curse on old Rodge. Like, a proper curse. She was going to come from beyond the grave and hunt him down. Speaking in tongues, I'm telling you.' he embellished with a little laugh.

'I expect she was provoked.' commented Dennis Priest with a curl of the lip.

'Here, Roger.' called Maxine, seeing him come in. 'You want to be careful with that. I know someone who does exorcisms. You want a proper exorcism if you've had a curse put on you.'

Maxine was, without doubt, the hardest person Roger had ever met. Barely over five feet tall, with short but thick curly black hair, she always looked as though smoke was being blown into her face. The placement of her missing tooth, front and slightly to the left, seemed too perfectly in tune with her image to be mere accident, as was also true of the giant silver cross that hung from her neck, frequently catching the light and blinding anyone facing her. Maxine had joined the unit on its opening, having gained her interpersonal skills from working over the counter at the DSS office on the London Road, the one with the reinforced glass and the metal detectors on the door. Rumour had it she had turned down more than one income support request at gunpoint. What was certainly true was the pen profile given by one of her previous bosses as a reference for the job, in which he'd stated that Maxine had a problem with the word 'yes'. That's what had landed her the job.

Dennis Priest, on the other hand, had come across from social work to join the unit. Dennis cared, he read books, bought from the internet using the library budget, explaining the fundamental root causes of antisocial behaviour. Dennis bemoaned social exclusion and was committed to parapraxis over punitive action. He spent much of his time on council-funded courses, developing his extensive counselling skills, although opportunities for Dennis to apply them in the field were rare, as he was nearly always away on courses. When he wasn't on courses, he was off ill. Dennis had a migraine problem and bad feet. But he was still a member of the team and, as such, entitled to venture opinions on the others' methods.

'One of you lot will go too far one of these days.' he said. 'You'll cross that line. I just don't want to be around when it all kicks off.'

Mason made a face and gave Dennis a V-sign under the desk. Roger blinked. He knew Dennis of old, knew where they differed, but, more important, how they were the same. Just like Roger and Spence, he'd applied to the new Antisocial Behaviour Unit for precisely the reason that it was new. Jobs in an embryonic section could be fashioned to the individual's specifications; there were no prior expectations hauling you back, no five-star predecessor to emulate. You could position yourself as you wished, design your own quiet life. Until, as Spence had intimated yesterday, so much work was being produced that it couldn't be swerved any longer. Then maybe it was time to move on.

This lot represented half of the unit's workforce. The rest were out and about, cleaning the streets on overtime. In theory, they were all supposed to work in pairs, investigating claims of antisocial behaviour and administering ASBOs across the region. In practice, however, Dennis dodged the dirty work but that was OK as Maxine preferred to work alone. This was for the best. With the storm of volatility that surrounded her, it was difficult for any oppo to predict the next move. Her own sixth sense for trouble, honed to the sharpness of a syringe at the DSS, always kept her one step ahead. Maxine's usual tactic was to counter aggression with greater aggression, but she could get away with that among the chavs. She was, after all, one of them.

'Hey, Mason.' said Spence. 'You'll know. This job yesterday. As we were leaving, this bloke chased after us with a bat. He came out of this Mary Molloy's house and just before she was shouting for Shane. Any idea who it might have been?'

Mason cocked his head in thought, then widened his eyes. 'Tattoos?' he asked.

Spence smiled, nodded. 'Covered in them.'

Mason was impressed. 'Must be Shane Trickett. Heard of him?'

They weren't sure.

'Oh yeah. Shane Trickett. Serious contender. Very tasty. He used to live in that squat opposite the ice rink. They set fire to it when the eviction notice came down, nearly killed that Bangladeshi family upstairs.'

One or two of the others signalled a vague memory of this.

'Trickett did some time. But now.' Mason said with a groan, reaching down to pull something out of the bottom drawer of his desk, 'he's shacked up with Mary Molloy. Interesting.'

'Bet he's fiddling his housing benefit.' said Maxine, hunched over her timesheet, busy with a little flexitime fiction.

Mason sat himself back upright, holding a ledger. Opening it, he removed a piece of paper, which he put down on the desk. Unfolding it into A3 size, he began to add to the markings already on it, using a ruler to make a straight line at one point. This was Mason's tree of troublemakers, a diagrammatic web representing the complex interconnection among the antisocial classes. He claimed that it was a useful working tool, but the truth was that Mason's work also happened to be his hobby.

'There.' he said, completing the entry. 'Didn't Trickett used to live with one of the Donnelly sisters? Oof.' He made a face. 'She was on the ugly pills as well.'

Roger felt suddenly uncomfortable being there, out of sympathy with the jokey atmosphere. He felt like getting in the car and driving. Maybe this time he wouldn't turn off at the last junction.

A new presence, lanky and energetic, bustled into their corner of the large open-plan office. It was Fitch, clutching a black binder crammed with paper.

'Shite a light.' he said, throwing himself into one of the office chairs, crossing his long legs and starting to swivel fast. 'I need a drink. Social policy group meeting.' he explained, rubbing his face. 'Talk about an uphill struggle.'

Fitch was the acting head of the Antisocial Behaviour Unit. The 'acting' part, the qualification of his status, was there as a constant reminder to Fitch that he wasn't secure in his position, that there were doubts about him in certain quarters. Typically, though, Fitch revelled in it. As he liked to point out, he was 'acting' when everybody else was drowning in the treacle of 'social justice'.

For Fitch was messianic in his crusade against antisocial behaviour. He saw antisocial behaviour where nobody else did. In a now-famous mission statement, he had christened his philosophy as one of 'positive intolerance'. Fitch played the game of multi-agency meetings, policy roadshows and community consultation. He'd even recruited Dennis as a sop to his detractors, but the truth was that he measured success in numbers. Numbers of repossessions, injunctions and evictions. For Fitch held the position that every tenant had to spend today earning the right to stay housed tomorrow. Like the majority of positions he adopted, it was calculated to incite the ire of the woolly hats in Social Services, with whom he shared a mutual loathing. He revelled in the pariah status that he and his chosen band worked in, shunted into the dingiest corner of St Jude's House.

Dennis Priest looked up when he heard mention of the social policy group. 'I didn't know the group was meeting.' he said, clearly put out.

'Convened at short notice.' Fitch explained, rubbing a knuckle under his nose. 'It's the Shaughnessy case. They've still got—' he held up both hands and simulated inverted commas with both index fingers, shaking his head from side to side '—issues.'

The Shaughnessy affair was a cause célèbre, with Fitch hanging firm to his hard line. Declan Shaughnessy was a fifteen-year-old glue-sniffer and all-purpose delinquent who'd taken to systematically abusing a Pakistani newsagent on Transport Road who'd refused to sell him a pack of cigarettes. On one occasion, having raided the bins behind a nearby greengrocer, he had peppered Mr Ahmed's shop window with several bags full of rotting produce. A number of witnesses had seen this, and an ASBO was being aggressively sought against him, one of the conditions of which stated that Declan was forbidden from carrying any item of fruit or veg in a public space.

'They're still trying to get us to relax the fruit thing.' said

Fitch. 'But I said no. They even got some bloody Nazi up from public health. She said their five-a-day unit had advised her that it might constitute a breach of his human rights to deny him access to food with health-giving properties.'

'They could have a point.' Dennis proffered.

'Bollocks.' said Fitch. 'The only thing that little scrote would use a courgette for is to…never mind. They're living in a fantasy world up there. Anyway, I held firm. Fucking yoghurt knitters.' He stopped, turned to Roger. 'Rodge, I meant to say. Sorry about your dad, mate. Jesus, here's me waffling on. You need any time off…'

'Thanks.' said Roger. 'I'll let you know.'

'Free pass, you lucky bastard.' said Spence, careful to keep it out of earshot of Fitch, who had got up and was in the process of going into his adjacent private office. But something arrested him after a few paces. It took a moment for him to remember what it was, causing him to dig in his pocket for a set of keys.

'Yeah, shit, I knew there was something.' he said, turning back to address the assembled team. 'Sorry, guys, but I need someone to run over to Goossens…'

He held up a hand to stop the chorus of groans.

'Not Goebbels.' said someone.

'It's been empty for months.'

'It's condemned, innit?'

Fitch put up a hand.

'We've had some reports that kids have been breaking into the stairway.'

'And that's news?' asked Maxine.

'I said we'd check it out, maybe catch someone in the act. Who fancies it?'

There were no takers until Roger stood up. 'I'll go.'

'You sure?' Fitch asked him.

Roger nodded. Spence snorted.

'Bring them back in tomorrow.' said Fitch, throwing the keys across to him. Roger didn't make a clean catch, had to reach down to pick them off the floor. When he looked up, Spence was off his seat, peering down at him with a puzzled look.

'You all right?'

'Why?'

'You just volunteered for something.'

Roger felt irritated. This was typical of Spence, just going too far. The joke was wearing thin. He huffed to express his displeasure.

'Not now, OK?' he said, pulling his coat off the back of the chair. 'Not in the mood.'

'You can tell me.' he told Roger.

'Tell you what?'

Spence shrugged.

'The angle. I mean, Goebbels? Come on. There has to be an angle.'

But Roger was halfway out.

6

He drove for a couple of hours, happy to sit in the rush-hour traffic, staring into space. Having unconsciously negotiated himself into as many traffic logjams and bottle-necks as was possible in two hours, he eventually found himself faced with some freedom of movement. As with the night before, going home was an unsatisfactory option. But tonight he found himself with an alternative choice. Not much of a choice but a choice nevertheless.

So he made for the Composers' Estate. Having had no real intention of going there when he left the office, Roger found himself heading for Goossens House.

From the outset, the history of Goossens had been messy. The centrepiece of the Composers' redevelopment project, a classic gap-site mistake, it had originally been envisaged at some fifteen storeys high, but the planners cashed in on a sub-sidy-for-height arrangement with the government by bunging another ten on top. Built during an era of soaring inflation and piss-poor industrial relations, the cost had gone through the roof, even when there wasn't anything vaguely akin to a roof on it. By this time, completion of the Composers' and Goossens in particular had become a test of political will, even when the two chief building companies went bust and work was suspended for months, during which time half of what was standing was vandalised beyond repair. When work finally restarted, speed over safety became the quiet mantra. A dispute broke out between the final construction company and the council, who refused to foot the bill for additional costs. The builders had threatened to invoke a clause in the contract allowing them to sell the properties off into the private sector. The council had nowhere to go until some bright spark had suggested a counter-measure. As they retained the right to name the streets and buildings according to powers granted them in the bylaws, they threatened to christen the whole estate with names drawn from Third Reich infamy – hence Arne (formerly Himmler) Avenue, Vaughan Williams (formerly Belsen) Street, and, of course, Goebbels, a.k.a. Goossens. As a deterrent, it had worked. But to those who knew, the names stuck like gum to a pavement.

It was still light as Roger made the turn from the road that skirted the Composers' on one side. As always, he knew a physical sensation on crossing the threshold, a tightening of valves all through his body, a squeezing inside. The baseball bat had it too, shivering on the back seat where it still lay as he hit one of the road bumps that had been put down to impede joyriders.

On either side of the road were long, very long five-storey point slab blocks: banks of flats in long rows, balconied walkways out front, dotted with numerous small windows. They didn't look too bad (only a few windows boarded up, even the odd set of tended curtains) but they had a sinister agenda, drawing you into the dark heart of the Composers' with a false sense of optimism. Once you reached their end, you came face to face with Goossens and the buildings that faced it, more slab blocks, shorter and flatter and sitting on low stilts, stretched out like acolyte insects in supplication around a large open area paved in concrete slabs. At various, apparently random, points across the plain's surface, architectural furniture adorned it – a cracked pebble-dash bench here, a hexagonal planter frothing with rubbish there, a sequence of concrete bollards with the tops lopped off. This space had been given the title of 'piazza' in the giddy days of its design and the name had lingered as a dark joke.

Even on a cloudy day like this, Goossens cast a long shadow across it.

Formed of a dark, unshining brick, the building rose upwards from the ground and encompassed a jutting space between right and left, impossible to define in terms of shape. On a central high-rise block, living spaces were recessed behind high stone balconies which reminded Roger of the sacks pelicans carry their food in. A number of small windowless connections containing deck-accessed flats attached themselves to a narrower, tubular structure that stood adjacent, like a calliper keeping a limb straight. This was the shaft, originally designed for a lift but altered to steps as a cost-cutting measure, most likely where the problem kids had got into the building. On the opposite side of the main block, a number of downward loops attached themselves to the building like dirty mug handles. These were the other outer stairs, highly unsafe but handy as escape routes between floors should the need arise. Other external stairwells and walkways littered the outer surface of the building, coming from nowhere and leading nowhere, as though smacked on by a child.

To call Goossens ugly was inappropriate. It went beyond aesthetics. It was insane but not in a flighty, crazy way. Every time Roger saw it, he felt a little closer to its meaning.

It was clinical depression made flesh.

The usual mixture of anecdote and experience had taught Roger not to leave his car parked anywhere adjacent to the piazza. During daylight, it was only as dodgy as anywhere else but night fell quicker on the Composers' than was the case elsewhere. Roger drew the motor around the back of the building, to a dead space once designed for rubbish collection but in fact ideal for drug-taking and glue-sniffing, now fenced off by giant gates three times Roger's height.

Nobody around. He attacked the padlock on the gate with the bundle of keys Fitch had given him. A large, Hammer Horror one did the trick and Roger drove the motor in, locking the gate again behind him. Away to his right, on the opposite side to Goossens' rear end, ran the canal. A monument to greater days of industrial activity, this final stretch of the waterway had largely fallen into disuse. One of the countless half-baked ideas behind the Composers' genesis had been that of revitalising the canal, of bringing people closer to it. Inevitably, a couple of unaccompanied toddlers got too close to it and met their fate, persuading the council to quickly knock up a breeze-block wall that looked better after it had been graffitied than it did before. There were only a couple of access points through, making it a godsend for the glue-sniffers and drug-takers and their insatiable appetite for Lebensraum. But things had turned very nasty when a vogue developed for attacking the few remaining vessels that used the canal, the desperate young men of the Composers' jumping on to boats as they passed under the walkway bridges dotting its length. After one robbery and sustained sexual assault on a holiday barge that had missed its turn north into friendlier country, they'd just padlocked shut all access from the estate once and for all. Very occasionally, a coughing barge, black with soot, would saunter past, laden with old tyres, the brace of crewmen standing on deck holding dogs on leashes and carrying metal bin lids to protect them from the stones the kids liked to throw at it from over the wall.

Having secured the gate behind him, Roger returned to the car and pulled out the baseball bat, letting it rest gently against the palm of his free hand for a moment. His sudden owner-ship of it smacked of serendipity.

Two more padlocks and a deadbolt later, Roger stood inside Goossens once more, at the bottom of a stairway, eyes scanning, nostrils flaring at the smell of piss, as if piss was infused into the concrete steps, as if gallons of dark yellow piss had been used to mix the cement itself. He could hear noises, or rather *feel* them, like creaking in a joint. Ahead of him was a staircase, to his left another door.

He had entered at a mezzanine level between basement and ground floor, the walls stained with tidemarks from the big flood a few years back. Roger didn't like the silence. He started up the stairs, holding the bat loosely, letting it scrape the stone.

The linoleum floor on the ground-floor reception area looked squeaky, as it probably had the first day that Goebbels' first intake of disbelieving pensioners and young parents had gleefully taken possession of their new dream homes in the sky. Across at the far side, Roger could see the pulled-down shutters of the concierge's office. Roger remembered the way that the very word was used like a talismanic incantation, a prophecy of success. A building with a caretaker would prob-ably fall down, but a *concierge* would ensure it immortality. The first holders of the post were figures of respect; they actually held qualifications earned over a couple of weekends at com-munity college. As things deteriorated, however, the selection process became less stringent and the most important attribute for new applicants was the ability to 'handle yourself'. When Goossens opened, there had been three concierges. By the end there was only one, an itinerant Irishman called Norman whom Roger had got to know quite well. In truth, Norman's appointment was only semi-official – he was given a free apartment on the empty first floor in lieu of payment and lived off his merchant navy pension. In return, he donned the chemical suit every other day and did his bit to keep the one working lift excrement-free. It was during the Composers' 'riot' of 1995 (in truth, more of a midsummer punch-up that the coppers had decided to escalate for their own amusement) that Norman had been targeted as an authority figure. His flat had come under attack and he was forced to board himself up in the bathroom. It was only with the help of half a dozen helmeted, plastic-shielded officers that Norman was hustled away from Goebbels once and for all, like the last troop out of Saigon.

Roger bypassed the first two floors on his ascent. The first-floor flats were larger than the rest; they had been specifically altered to accommodate the large families who had moved in during the great second migratory wave and the point of no return for Goossens. As he climbed, Roger couldn't help but marvel at Goossens' accelerated progress from dream to dereliction. From his days as a housing officer, he knew that every wrong turn that could be made had been, almost in textbook fashion. A Bison Wall-frame construction given the green light years after the first serious doubts about the system had been aired, Goossens' very design was a fuck-up. Roger remembered enough from his housing manuals to still cite the raft of mistakes that the whole estate exhibited: poor spacial organisation, confused space, overhead walkways encouraging ejectamenta, interconnecting exits, interconnecting vertical routes, hidden entrances encouraging urine and faeces – you name it. But that stuff was normal. Not even that could entirely explain Goossens' spectacular demise.

It had all started with one six-year-old girl who tried to imitate a pigeon she'd seen perched on the railings of her family's eighteenth-floor flat. Suddenly everyone with children wanted to get down, or preferably out. Council promises of renovation were ignored and any number of families were rehoused back at ground level where they'd come from. Which left empty flats all over the building, now deemed unsuitable for any young families. The housing department decided on a policy of carefully spreading some of the council's more difficult tenants around the building in the hope that their behaviour would be elevated in the presence of more responsible neighbours. Fat fucking chance. Looking back, Roger felt the die had been cast the day the Clamm family had turned up with their trio of bull mastiffs and their cannibal car business.

Roger could remember the climate of fear from his early days with the council, climbing the same stairs (the lift bust) and waiting outside complainants' flats as they undid the half-dozen safety locks from inside. The lifts had been the first to go, then the laundry rooms in the basement (which you couldn't get to without the lifts, anyway) became no-go areas, followed by the terrace on the roof. Even so, it was only when a binman was attacked and thrown twelve storeys down an internal chute that Goossens started to become infamous. The rest of the refuse collectors refused to pick up from the building and bags of garbage regularly began sailing down through the night sky. Other tenants weren't waiting, they were simply leaving, preferring homelessness. So more empty flats, which is when the nutters and the smackheads started moving in, initially as squatters but simply allowed to stay. The first in a spate of suicides followed, then came the riots, then the flooding caused by abuse of the fire hoses, then the fire on the upper floors which, without hoses, there was no way of stopping until three more residents met their ends at the hands of the Goossens' curse. And that's what it was. Everything but a plague of fucking locusts until even the Clamms decided it was too dangerous and it had been emptied, with most people still there relocated elsewhere on the Composers'. That had been eighteen months ago. There had been talk of demolition, but with the building wedged into so tight a space that would require the assistance of the local community in a temporary evacuation and, as most people commented, when was the last time those maniacs had gone along with anything the council asked?

Only when he got up there did Roger remember about the third floor.

Seeing the carnage, Roger couldn't help but smile. Here before him was the most ruthless deconstruction of the hubris that lay in Goossens' conception. Oh yes indeed, they had been asking for it.

Roger pushed the door open and went in.

It was constituted of one large room, free of the pillars in the vestibule. A giant expanse from wall to wall to wall, envisaged as a communal space for the inhabitants to come together in and share, a glorified TV room. By Roger's time in Housing, it had already become a no-go area. Roger had seen photographs of it after it had first been built. In the photos, contemporary furniture had been pushed up against the walls, two polo-necked male models stood at a small bar area, being served coffees by a smiling young woman, who'd presumably just left her young children to swing from the balcony rails on the tenth floor. There was even, Roger remembered, a fucking piano. The third floor had been a key weapon in the 'selling' of Goossens with absurd fantasies of community, as if it were the exercise yard in a prison you could have a cappuccino and a quick singsong in before locking yourself away again in your low-ceilinged cell twelve floors up.

Instead, the inhabitants of Goossens had used it to house the one thing they cultivated in abundance.

Rubbish.

Like the lift shafts and the laundry chutes, the third floor had been co-opted as a tipping site, one giant stationary skip. Larger objects, like furniture, tumble dryers and, inevitably, a couple of supermarket trolleys, punctuated the general ankle-high mess of clothing, broken toys and soil. The lift doors on to the third floor had been welded shut, and the hatches on the bar area were down hard, sporting some unoriginal graffiti.

There was one feature, however, that remained intact.

The third floor was walled on three sides. The remaining edge comprised one giant sheet of reinforced glass, ten feet high by maybe fifty across. It had been, at the time, a revolutionary design with a fibre matrix, inspired by anti-terrorist technology, and was riskily declared as being unbreakable. Roger was sure plenty of Goebbels' finest had put this to the test but it had held firm while much had crumbled around it. Negotiating the minefield of junk until he stood on the aircon grilles that lay on the floor right next to it, he put his palms on the window and looked out over the piazza. With years of experience on this site, it dawned on Roger that he hadn't ever been particularly aware of this window when looking from the outside. But that was because it had been designed that way – it was just far enough away not to interest the vandals outside and, although you could peer out on the vistas beneath, from down there nobody could see in. A voyeur's paradise.

The window faced into the heart of the Composers', overlooking the piazza and the other smaller and equally complex buildings that seemed to be bowing in Goebbels' thrall – Grainger House, Elgar House, Bax Villas.

In the small, rusting playground at the corner of the piazza, two boys, looking about seven or eight, the hair on the crown of both their heads stuck up like feathers, were attacking the seats on the seesaw with large linked chains that had once held up the toddler swings. Fifty yards away, a girl in a pink tracksuit sat with sexual sloth on the unbroken end of an asphalt bench while her friend, a doughnut of blubber pushed down by the tightness of her tank top, cycled around her on a bike far too small. The cyclist's furious little pedalling motions were quite comical but she lost control and ran straight into the bench-dweller, who slapped her hard across the back of the head with her state-of-the-art third-generation WAP phone.

Across at the bottom of Bax Villas, almost hidden under a concrete canopy, several children milled around the front of the estate's one remaining store. Even in the short time Roger and the others had been working in the Antisocial Behaviour Unit, Pandy's Handy had been the reluctant engine behind more ASBOs than any other establishment. Why Pandy Patel still bothered was beyond everybody's comprehension, but he clung on in the misplaced hope of better days or, even less likely, a compulsory purchase. Roger pictured him inside, behind the mesh he had had to put up over the counter, smiling in hope and fear at his own clientele. Pandy's problem was that he had to live on the estate as well, in Delius Grove, so he couldn't risk provoking the ire of the Dolkins or the Moriartys by insisting their kids paid for things. They could effectively nick as much of his dwindling stock as they wanted. It was only when the serious threats of violence came in that he felt compelled to ring the police. In truth, Fitch was the biggest nuisance in Pandy's life. He was for ever trying to calm Roger's boss down in his incontinent ASBO distribution.

'Makes my life bloody difficult.' he had often quietly complained via the department's recorded message line. 'All I want is a quiet life. Call off your dogs, man.'

And, right now, at a little before seven, it was quiet. Quiet by the Composers' standards. But standing above, overlooking the whole area, Roger could feel the heat welling up inside Elgar, Grainger and the others, a rumble in the superstructure that would spill out after nightfall, as it nearly always did. As long as it didn't rain.

He felt something of the excitement of the place.

And from here you could see everything.

Roger scuttled back down the steps to his car. At the back of the building he remained unseen as he opened the boot and took out his dad's anglepoise lamp and a travel rug. Back upstairs and in the faint light, Roger kicked, dragged and pushed enough of the rubbish out of the way to locate an electric socket a few feet away from the window. In among the discarded items, Roger had spied an abandoned leather armchair, shiny and black, with giant flat arms big enough for a medium-sized dog to lie comfortably. The seat cushion had two big Stanley knife scars and an unidentified black tacky substance on it, but Roger folded the travel rug up a couple of times and laid it on top.

The power was still on and the anglepoise gave the glowing gloom a tint of colour. Roger sat down, adjusted the position of the chair a couple of times and began to watch.

Things started slowly, the activity scattered in small pockets, like the proceedings on stage during the overture of an opera. As the light faded further the bored children, with their sudden, spastic acts of violence, subtly gave sway to older adolescents and their more sustained, less fluctuating level of aggression. Any younger ones who lingered were treated with disdain and relieved of any possessions. One girl of six watched in tears as her bike was systematically destroyed by a group of teenagers, led by one who Roger deduced was her own brother. Quickly aware that her anguish was only an incentive for them to continue, she resolved the situation by joining in herself. Roger looked on with a sense of privilege at witnessing this rite of passage. Until this point, antisocial activity existed only in a dry report, in an incoherent complaint, or an exaggerated anecdote. To see it first hand, to see cause and effect evinced with such clarity, had a profound effect on Roger. There was a simple perfection in this drama acted out solely for his benefit. Something in it moved him.

As the adolescents imposed themselves on the piazza, the

fractured collective began to merge into a single pack of anything between twenty and thirty. Around a central core of some half a dozen key personalities, the others would circulate like electrons flirting with the heart of an atom. The group was in constant loose-limbed action, their exaggerated motions amplified by the clothes worn by both sexes, tight above the waist and loose below. They all wore baseball caps. As they moved together around the piazza, sharing cans of PoundBlaster own-brand lager and swinging with artless sexuality from the playground ruins, arguments or manic group hilarity flared up instantaneously, with no obvious provocation for either. On a couple of occasions, elderly passers-by were targeted for abuse and irritation on the way to and from Pandy's shop. The trek out after dark was made only in the direst of needs. One old dear in a Mobility wheelchair tried to keep a brave face as her progress was hindered, implying that boys will be boys and it was all a bit of harmless fun. Roger imagined the back story, the sinking of her heart on discovering she was out of milk or cat food and would have to brave a trip outside. It cost her most of the contents of her purse to be given access back to Grainger.

In the absence of outsiders, the group turned in on itself. The fattest male began to be targeted, had his mobile phone taken from him and stamped on. As he tried to collect it from the ground, one of the girls, a cigarette hanging from her mouth, gave him a hard kick in the ribs. Getting back up, the little fatty gave her a push and was set on by three other boys, who wrestled him to the ground and stripped him of virtually all his clothing. Even then, back on his feet in nothing but a giant pair of fake Calvin Kleins, watching his attire being set fire to in a dustbin, he was reluctant to leave the group. What awaited him at home was probably ten times worse.

The baseball caps were gradually being replaced by

drawn-up hoods as the average age began to creep up. The sexually precocious girls lingered after their male contemporaries had been scared off to engage in public foreplay before retiring between the concrete stilts of Elgar and Grainger for possible consummation.

Slowly, Roger sensed the mood on the piazza changing to something harder, more determined. An influx of young men began to populate the piazza, disgorged from cars coming in from outside the Composers'. Thumping bass throbbed through the night, even permeating through the glass of Roger's eyrie.

This was a time for trade, the atmosphere tense and businesslike as nefarious transactions were undertaken, only for most of the produce to then be consumed quite openly on the benches. The estate smackheads, not an insignificant caucus on the Composers', would appear only to make a purchase before scuttling away to indulgence. Then, as the mood mellowed, more of the Composers' women emerged to join their menfolk. The pulse of the car stereos caused one or two stringy couples to start tentatively dancing around an upside-down moped that had been set on fire. One of the women took pleasure in throwing vodka on the flames to make them surge upwards. When the fuel tank went up, it seemed to come as a surprise. One of the bystanders was hurt by something flying from the debris and he retired to a bench, bleeding from the head. Agitated mobile phone calls followed. The pushers got in their cars and scarpered but there was no need for them to rush. The ambulance, if it was coming, would be a while. Roger knew what the problem was. The emergency services were as wise to the Composers' as everybody else. Notwithstanding the fact that four out of five calls from that location proved to be hoaxes, venturing into the Composers' was as dangerous for them as anybody else. When it did arrive, it came with a police escort and with a fire engine in tow.

Police, fire and ambulance. The Triple Crown. Good going for a Tuesday night, even on the Composers'.

First, there were the recriminations over the delay. The paramedics were harangued on their way to the injured man who, when they finally reached him, was more than reluctant to put out his cigarette or drop his can of PoundBlaster Premium Brew. When they tried to take him into the ambulance, he went ballistic and sent a WPC flying. With the coppers engaged in containing him and the firemen putting out the moped embers, the others decided to have a little fun. Scuttling up the ladders on its side, one couple got on top of the fire engine and began pulling off their clothes to concerted applause from below. A few others sneaked in the back of the ambulance and had a rummage through the first-aid cabinets. Looking for morphine, Roger assumed, beginning to feel a little tired. Not the usual, empty tiredness, but the fulfilling tiredness that comes with achievement. The battered armchair was surprisingly comfortable. As the emergency vehicles slowly left the piazza to a shower of stones and broken bottles, Roger felt himself hauled down into sleep by the calm rhythm of the flashing lights, yellow and blue, yellow and blue…

He woke up in the chair, hungry but refreshed. Checking the time, he calculated that he'd slept for nine hours. He got up and stretched, moving closer to the window. Rolling his shoulder a couple of times, he realised that it felt much better. Blinking hard, he also knew that the itchiness in his eye had gone.

Below him, all was calm. It was a bright morning. Even over the Composers' there was an intangible optimism in the air of a new day. Roger saw the small, wiry figure of Pandy standing outside his shop, smoking a fag and surveying the empty piazza. For a short moment he even looked a little proud.

But fantasies of community were easier when there was nobody around. The hopes of the morning were illusory, for night would come again.

Roger headed out, taking the bat with him, but leaving the anglepoise and the blanket where they were.

For next time.

7

They drove, the three of them, from the funeral in silence. Nick sat a long way back, almost fully reclined in the passenger seat, Marion in the back just where she could be seen in the rear-view mirror, staring wistfully out of the window. Beth had started to cry about her biology revision and Roger had excused her from having to come.

He was glad it was over. He had to admit he could see the appeal of the idea of the humanist funeral his father had always insisted on, but the reality was rather chilling. But perhaps it was fitting that his father's send-off had the atmosphere of a town council meeting, with a few old, bent former comrades prepared to stand up, lean on the rail ahead of them and defend his memory in debating tones. They used words like 'committed', 'resolute' and even 'stoical'.

Roger had contemplated standing up himself. It seemed only right that there should be a contribution from the front row where the three of them, the only family members, were sitting. He tried quickly to prepare a generous speech in his head. But in thinking of how to describe Dad as a father, all he could come up with was 'committed' and 'stoical'. So when the last speaker had sat down, Roger had sat through the long silence, somehow feeling it was his father's last, calculated act of awkwardness. He had already resolved not to offer an open invitation to the mourners and persuaded Marion against preparing any food, not even just in case.

Roger had to concentrate on the drive home. His instinct was to head somewhere else, one place in particular, but his whispered discussion with Marion on the front row while Nick was away in the toilet had ended in a promise.

'I know it's been a difficult time for you.' she had told him in a blend of sympathy and steeliness she had perfected over time, 'and I'm not going to ask where you're going every night until the small hours…'

Roger was aware of his eyes dancing.

'…Sometimes you're not coming back at all. I can hear you sneaking in first thing, pretending you've slept in the spare room when you haven't.' She took a deep breath. 'I just think you owe it to us to…whenever you've dealt with whatever issues you've got…I'll cook a nice dinner tonight. The kids want to see you. Will you promise to stay?'

'Of course.' Roger had said. Now, turning on to their street, he was regretting it. After all, tonight was Friday night. There was bound to be something worth seeing on the piazza tonight.

Roger was the last one to see the parcels. Nick had sat up from his recumbent position with a puzzled look.

'Must be a mistake.' Marion had ventured on seeing them.

By the time Roger had got out of the car, Marion was already proved wrong. She and Nick were poring over the dozen or so boxes that had been left on their doorstep.

'But they're all addressed to you.' Marion told him.

Roger tightened the edges of his mouth and nodded. He had recognised the CostBlast motif on the largest box.

'So what's in them?' Nick wanted to know.

Roger shrugged. 'I'm not sure.'

'What do you mean?' Marion asked, the first flicker of hysteria in her eye. 'How can you not know?'

'I can't honestly remember.' answered Roger, a little pained. 'We can just stick them in the garage.'

Nick wasn't having it. 'I want to open them up.'

'You bought all this?' Marion asked. 'What for?'

Roger couldn't give her an answer.

Marion was glancing around, clearly concerned about the neighbours having witnessed the delivery. 'Why were they left outside?' she wanted to know. 'Why didn't Beth take them inside?'

Nick sniggered. 'Oh, didn't she mention that she was heading over to Marcus Carr's for some work on the finer points of human biology? Don't you want to see what's in here?' Nick asked, picking up three of the smaller packets and taking them into the house.

A question struck Marion as she looked up in horror.

'This isn't…filth, is it?'

'Don't think so…Tat would be nearer the mark.'

She shook her head, tried to gather herself. 'For God's sake, let's get this stuff out of sight.'

By the time Roger got all the boxes into the lounge, Nick had already got through the duct tape on his first and was flipping it open.

'What's this shit?' he asked, pulling out a few CD cases.

'Oh yeah.' Roger said, falling on to the settee. Now he remembered the twenty-CD set of country-and-western legends they'd convinced him to buy.

A disappointed Nick had moved on to another, larger parcel when Marion came in and surveyed the scene. Roger wanted her to get into the spirit of it, to just sit down and start opening boxes, like it was Christmas morning.

But she only looked on as Nick started pulling out and holding up a number of rough-looking towels in a variety of sizes.

'What colour is that?' she asked.

'Pistachio.' Roger recollected. 'They said it would go with any colour.'

'It's foul.'

'Big saving.' Roger replied.

There was a pause, broken first by Nick's sniggering. 'Bad taste is in, Mum. Go with it.'

'Someone's got to pay for this?' she said, pointing at Nick's next discovery. 'What are they?'

'Hold it up.' Roger asked Nick, screwing up his face at a nasty short-sleeved shirt with collar. 'Golfwear.' he explained.

'You don't play golf.'

'Might take it up.'

'They're all extra large.' commented Nick, puzzled.

'Yeah, that was the only size they had.' Roger explained sheepishly, remembering his arousal at the sight of Lorraine, his favourite CostBlast model, sporting one with her hip stuck provocatively outwards, her long straight hair cascading down her shoulder, her slatternly look straight at him...

'You'll be sending all this rubbish back?' Marion wanted to know.

Roger sighed. That seemed like a lot of effort. 'It was just a bit of fun.' he said, calling to Marion as she left the room. 'I got you a foot spa!'

Nick was looking at him.

'What?' he wanted to know.

'All this. It's mad, Dad.' Nick said. Roger couldn't tell if his tone was supportive or admonishing.

'There's some Playstation stuff in one of them.' he told him, getting up. 'Set the thing up. We'll have a game of it.'

'Where you going?'

'Get a drink.'

Nick's genetic sensitivity to his father's moods gave him some hope in trying it on.

'Can I have one?'

'Sure. What do you want?'

'Whatever you're having.'

Roger found himself vaguely disappointed that Marion wasn't in the kitchen as he poured decent slugs of gin into the two glasses. Yes, giving him a drink was probably the wrong thing to do but the kid wanted a drink, so let him have a drink. It was technically a wake anyway, but Roger wanted to show her how easy it was to break the rules, to *change* the rules. That you didn't have to live *by the rules.* So many fucking rules. Dad had more rules than anybody else. Now he was burned to a crisp and nobody cared.

He chucked in some ice and topped them up with the flat PoundBlaster tonic that had been there a long time. Normally he'd put in a lemon wedge but there was none to hand.

Roger took the drinks through and sat down on the floor next to Nick, who took his glass and sipped at it, trying not to make a face of displeasure at the taste. Roger bumped him gently with his shoulder and picked up his Playstation console.

'Come on then, hardknock.' he said. 'Prepare to get your arse kicked.'

'These games are kind of old.' Nick commented. 'Let's just play *War on Terror* again.'

'Whatever.' said Roger, draining half his gin and tonic in one go.

They started playing and Roger felt a strong sense of emotion towards his boy. He wanted them to be mates, he wanted them to have a good time. He didn't want to be judgemental.

Roger didn't feel like doing any *parenting.*

Roger had a nice buzz on by the time they sat down for dinner, but he was aware of an unsettled atmosphere around the others at the table. Beth had returned breezily only to be drawn into a furious row with her mother as to her behaviour in going out. Roger had wanted to tell Marion that it was OK, that Beth shouldn't be made to feel bad about not coming to Dad's funeral. He disagreed with Marion when he heard her accuse Beth of lying. She hadn't lied. She just hadn't told them. Two different things. He felt like he wanted to intervene but he couldn't quite drag himself away from *War on Terror II: Wind of Revenge* after he'd finally got on to level four after two hours of trying.

Nick, halfway through a second gin and tonic, face red, had just sniggered at the raised voices coming from upstairs.

'Man, someone needs to take a serious chill pill.'

'Chill pill.' Roger repeated with a laugh and a nod.

They had both looked up at the ceiling at the sudden descent of silence from upstairs.

Now, an hour and a half later, Beth, eyes still rimmed red from more tears, sat opposite her mother, her hands pulled hard into the sleeves of her sweater. Marion was serving food and making conversation but she had the air of someone kicking furiously below the waterline, only ever a moment from drowning.

'We can use the towels at the swimming baths, I suppose.' she was postulating. 'And Keith Eggham plays golf, doesn't he? Extra large might fit him. I can give the watch to Glenda for Christmas.'

Glenda was the cleaning lady, paid well under the minimum wage.

'So you're keeping the foot spa, then?' asked Roger.

Marion just stared down as she dolloped rice on to his plate. 'You want some more, Nicholas?'

Nick reached out to get it but his movement was a little uncontrolled. With the back of his hand he knocked over what remained of the glass of wine Roger had poured him (unremarked on by his mother, a sign to Roger that she was beginning to see the light).

'Oh.' inhaled Marion, quickly starting to dab it off the tablecloth.

'Sorry.' said Nick, sitting back and opening his eyes widely.

'What foot spa?' Beth wanted to know, breaking her silence.

'Dad bought loads of mad kit.' Nick explained, his voice unnecessarily raised. Roger couldn't help but smile at his son's appreciation.

'Nobody told me.' she said.

Nick blinked slowly and sat back. 'That's 'cause you weren't here, were you?'

Beth stared daggers at him. Roger sensed the spark between them, knew that it would be allowed full expression only away from here at some future point, far from him and Marion.

But Roger was curious. He wanted to see it, out in the open. After all, it was Friday night.

'I told Beth it was OK.' said Roger, over a mouthful. 'I said she didn't have to come. If this—' he waved his fork '—boy – Marcus, is it? – can help you with your revision, then it makes sense.'

Beth looked uneasy.

'So how did you know who I was with?'

'Nick told us, didn't he?' he asked Marion, pushing some more stir-fry into his mouth.

Beth looked at Nick. Nick looked at Roger. Roger looked at Marion, made a questioning face. Marion looked away.

'What?' Roger said.

'Cheers, Dad.' said Nick.

'Yeah, thanks.' agreed Beth. 'Thanks for letting me know what a snitching little shit my brother is.'

'Language.' protested Marion half-heartedly.

Roger shook his head. 'Ah, you shouldn't tell tales on people.' he told Nick, whose face clouded over with self-pity.

'Grass.' hissed Beth.

Nick folded his arms. 'I just can't stand the hypocrisy. All this talk about revision and you go and miss Grandad's funeral just so you can get busy with Marcus Carr.'

'I've been through all that with your sister.' Marion told him. 'The matter's closed.'

Roger feared that Marion's intervention might put an end to the conflict, but he needn't have worried. Both now seething with feelings of injustice, they were definitely up for a rumble.

'Oh yeah, the matter's closed.' Nick protested, reddening in the face and throwing his arms up in the air. 'Just let it go for the little princess. She can do anything she likes and get away with it.'

'So immature.' muttered Beth, turning the knife.

Nick's face tightened to a meanness Roger had never seen before.

'Yeah, maybe if *I* shagged around, I could be more mature like you.'

'Nick!' splurted Marion. 'That's a—'

'You are so pathetic. Mum, Dad, I've never—'

'Oh come on. Everyone knows you've shagged him.'

'Nick!' repeated Marion. 'I'm not going to sit here—'

'Everyone calls you a slut behind your back.'

'God, you are so sexually frustrated.' retorted Beth, volcanic with fury. 'Is that why you try to rape people?'

Nick spat out a derisive laugh and waved a dismissive hand at her, pushing his chair on to two legs and leaning back against the wall, something that Marion hated.

'No?' said Beth. 'I know all about it. Alison Graves? When you attacked her at that party when she was coming out of the toilet? Now she's in counselling. Did you know that?'

Marion got up and began clearing plates. The accuracy of Beth's attack was self-evident as Nick swayed gently in his precarious position, staring at Beth and shaking his head.

'You are so dead.' he told her.

'Rapist.'

'Slut.'

'Stop it!' begged Marion, to Roger's irritation.

'I am not a slut.'

'So what else do you call it when you let a prole like Marcus Carr slip it to you?'

'Roger!' insisted Marion. 'Will you do something about these two? I can't bear it.'

But Roger was fixated.

'You're just a liar.' sneered Beth.

'He told everyone at school that you fucked him!'

Marion moaned.

'It's a lie.'

Nick let his chair rock slowly forward until he was sitting on four legs again. Marion glanced at them both in the brief silence. Believing, hoping that the worst was over, she started carrying the dishes towards the sink.

But Nick had one more nuke to drop.

'If it's a lie.' he asked quietly, 'then how come you're on the pill?'

The plates hit the kitchen floor with more force than mere gravity. Marion shrieked. 'WHAT?'

She wasn't heard by her children, who simply sat, staring each other out.

'I found them in your bedside table.' Nick added, unprovoked, but with what Roger thought sounded like the first hint of apology.

Roger saw that Nick was looking a little peaky. Seeing him in profile, he detected a few beads of sweat prominent on his forehead. After the G&Ts, Nick had been the one to call an end to the Playstation competition, saying he wanted a bath. Roger had seen him sneak upstairs with a couple of cans of beer in the half-hour before dinner. Now the glass and a half of wine were having an effect.

Beth got up with an air of exhaustion, looked across at her mother, who was squatting over the broken crockery, sobbing uncontrollably, with a look of sympathy and walked out.

Breathing deeply through his nose, Roger got up from the table and stooped to join Marion at her level. He put an arm on her shoulder.

'Come on.' he said. 'Leave them. Let's have a drink.'

With a wail she slid away from his hand and rushed out. Roger watched her go. He stood up again and chucked what he had picked up straight in the bin.

'I don't suppose you wanted to know any of that.' slurred Nick.

Roger thought about it as he ran himself a glass of water from the tap.

'What I want…You know what it is?' he mused. 'Everyone, your mum, you, your sister, you all seem…What I really want, more than anything else, is for you all to be happy.'

Nick looked across at him, glassy-eyed. 'Hey, Dad, you know something…?'

'What's that, mate?'

Nick's expression changed suddenly.

'Oh fuck. I think I'm going to be sick…'

Roger shut the door behind him, allowing his son some privacy as he retched over the kitchen sink.

Roger watched an hour of CostBlast with interest but no urge to buy. His favourite, Lorraine, was on, doing an early shift, modelling watches and sunglasses with a slovenly grace Roger found irresistible. Lorraine let it be known during the stream of chatter between her and the show's host that she was going out later, 'on the razz'.

Friday night, thought Roger ruefully as he turned the TV

off. Not even ten o'clock and the house was quiet, everyone in their bedrooms suffering in their different ways. Only Roger, he felt, was out of the loop of misery. He was through it and on the other side, where they would do better to join him.

Roger climbed the stairs purposefully and made for Marion's bedroom. *His* bedroom as well, he reminded himself.

He entered, making no attempt to be unnecessarily quiet. Marion had taken a long bath to relax and the air was heady with the smell of her balms. Roger quickly undressed and slid into bed, lying on his back next to her.

'Awake?' he asked her.

'Not asleep, if that's what you mean.'

'How you feeling?'

'I don't know what's happened to this family, Roger. I don't know if I can cope with all this. Especially when I feel like I'm dealing with it all on my own.' she told him, threatening to start crying with the last three words.

'You're not alone. OK, it's been an unusual time. But I stayed, like you asked me to. Now I've come into bed, like you asked me to.'

'That was before.'

'Let's concentrate on now.'

'You mean the now where your son's a pervert and your daughter sleeps around?'

Roger sighed, rolled on to his side and placed a hand on the soft swell of Marion's stomach.

'They're just doing what kids everywhere are doing.'

'And you find that reassuring?'

After a pause, Roger said: 'Yes, I do. I'm glad they're normal. And anyway.' he added, letting his fingers gently knead the flesh below her navel, 'why should they be having all the fun? Why shouldn't we get some too?'

Marion clicked her tongue, half turned away.

'Hey.' Roger said, pulling her back towards him with her

hand. He reached across and searched for her mouth with his.

'No.' she said.

Roger decided to persist.

'It'll do you good.' he said, trying to kiss her again and sending down a hand in what he hoped was tender exploration. 'You need to relax.'

'I don't want to be touched.'

Her body stiffened as his fingers moved inside the waist of her pyjamas.

'Stop it.'

Roger chose to see if he could ride out the resistance. His hand went deeper, tried to navigate a route down that wasn't there.

'No!' she shouted.

'Come on.' Roger tried. 'Let's live a little.'

'Get off me!' she cried, squirming away and off the bed, then pointing to the door. 'And get out!'

Roger heard someone come out on to the landing outside.

'Mum?' called Beth. 'You all right?'

He switched on the bedroom light.

'Marion?'

'I mean it! Get out!'

Roger picked up his clothes and exited, almost knocking over Beth, who was standing outside, close to the door.

'What's going on?' she asked.

'I'm popping out.' Roger replied.

He went straight to the bathroom to collect his toothbrush and shaving equipment before leaving, pausing only to take a dressing gown off the back of the door and gently drape it over Nick, who was lying on the floor where he'd fallen asleep, head near the toilet.

8

A MONTH LATER

Roger sat in the office, looking out on a bright but cold spring afternoon. He felt OK, fitter with cycling into work every day now that he'd let Marion keep the car, even though it had meant lifting out the boxes of Dad's books from their temporary home in the boot. He liked the new routine he'd created for himself. The office shower couldn't always be trusted to be hot and having to share it with unspecified others wasn't ideal but he was used to it now. He was used to a whole new life now.

Which was why speaking to Marion on the phone was unsettling him.

'I thought we'd been burgled.' she told him. 'If you're going to come into the house, the least you can do is let me know.'

'I just went to get some clothes.' he explained, to be met with silence. 'So, how are the kids?' he asked her.

'I went with Beth to see the doctor, then he spoke to me alone.'

'What did he say?'

'I don't think he took it seriously. He told me that young people were going to have sex, whatever happened.'

'He could have a point.'

'OK, let's just talk about something else, can we?'

Easier said than done. Finally, she said: 'There's some post here for you. Would you like me to forward it?'

'Sure. Send it to me here.'

'What's wrong with your home address?'

'It's OK. The office is fine.'

'Are you even going to tell me where you're staying? What if something happens? I need to know where you're living.'

'I'm just between places at the minute. Send it here. Is Nick around?'

He spoke briefly to his son, who couldn't quite hide his pleasure at being from what was now technically a broken home. Roger didn't blame him for that. He understood that it would do wonders for his kudos at school, might even do the trick with the Alison girl he'd tried it on with at the party.

He hung up and surveyed the room. Mason was there, writing up another knockabout visit he'd done earlier that afternoon. So, inevitably, was Dennis Priest. Dennis was eating a banana and sitting back in his specially ordered, ergonomically designed chair, his neck supported with an inflatable pillow like those used on long-haul flights. Dennis was thus signalling the onset of a migraine and an early departure from work. He was flicking through the local authority newsletter, silently aggrieved at something until he saw Roger was off the phone.

'Here, Rodge.' he asked. 'You don't think I'm a working-class traitor, do you?'

'Who called you a working class traitor?'

'That Hermione on the Homeless Working Group. Me, of all people?'

'Yeah.' said Mason, without looking up. 'When were you

ever working class?'

Dennis ignored him. 'I'm the one who set up the Homeless Liaison Forum...'

'Quality doss, that.' chimed in Mason.

'...I'm the only one who understands the impact of eviction on vulnerable groups in this community. You try to be constructive and all they do is call you a traitor to your class and accuse you of – what was it—"orchestrating a campaign of state oppression through harassment laws".'

Mason looked up. 'Makes it sound more of a laugh than it is.'

'I mean, I fully understand people's concerns about the legislation…'

'Like what?'

'Like the day we start seeing orders used to gag political dissent.'

Mason tapped the file he was working on.

'I hardly see how shitting through your neighbour's skylight is political dissent.'

Dennis scowled. He turned the page and something caught his eye.

'This will interest you, Roger.' he said, tapping the page with the back of his hand. 'You know Goossens of old.'

Roger didn't like the question. He felt his ears redden.

'You cut your teeth there, didn't you?' asked Dennis, keen to cement some kind of connection that might exclude Mason. 'I remember being at a couple of meetings with you on it. Must have been—' he leaned back in his chair with a smile '—Christ, I don't know, '86, '87. Have a look.' he said, throwing the newsletter over. It snagged on the air halfway across and fell at Roger's feet. Leaning down, he picked it up and folded it back. The picture was undoubtedly of Goossens House, although it was taken from an unfamiliar angle.

Dennis shook his head. 'Different times.' he added ruefully

with a smile. 'There were some good people on that residents' committee in those days. Committed people, people who took an interest...'

But Roger had tuned out from Dennis's bogus recollections. He read the headline and the first paragraph of the story with increasing horror before getting up, grabbing his coat and walking straight out.

He'd tracked Spence down on his mobile phone after more than an hour of trying to get through. When he finally did so, he was relieved to hear that Spence was still in the building, up in the canteen on the fifth floor. Not trusting St Jude's mischievous lifts, he ran up the stairs to find him sitting alone, the canteen staff closing up around him as he put the finishing touches to the private sale of a supply of geraniums that were deemed surplus to the City in Bloom stock.

'Yeah...' he was saying into the phone. 'Let me worry about that...I know what everyone is saying about Pease but we can get around that...Always...of course. Ciao.'

But the smile dropped from his face as he ended the call. Roger sat down quickly, leaned over the table.

'You have to help me with something.'

Spence was impassive. 'Listening.'

'It's Goossens.'

Spence shook his head. 'Goebbels? What of it?'

Roger handed him the newsletter, tapped the photo of the building with his knuckle.

'They want to knock it down.'

Spence cocked his head. Roger referred back to the paper. 'Pease...'

Spence tutted. 'Don't mention that name.'

'He's contracted DemoRent to handle the tricky knock-downs. They're going to do Goebbels as a starter.'

'It's about time, isn't it?'

Roger drew the back of his hand across the underside of his nose. 'They can't knock it down. It's not...They can't knock it down.'

Spence's brow furrowed. 'What's this? You getting all nostalgic for the shitholes of your youth? The place is a khazi. We spent years dreaming of seeing it down.'

'It's different now.'

'It's empty now, that's all. They should have blown it up when all those knackers were still living there. Better late than never.'

'You don't understand. They can't knock it down.' He paused, bit his bottom lip. 'I'm living there.'

Spence sat back, eyes wide, just as one of the canteen staff brought him over a freshly cooked plate of fish and chips. Only Spence got waitress service in the canteen.

'Thanks, Doreen, love.' He waited for her to be far enough away before leaning back towards Roger. 'You're living there? What do you mean, living there?'

'I mean it's where I go. Where I stay.'

Spence got serious in a hurry. 'So what, you got thrown out of the house? What happened?'

'Things weren't working out. I left.'

'You left to go and live in Goebbels?'

Roger nodded. Spence, uncharacteristically, put a hand on his shoulder. 'This is bad news, mate. I'm sorry. I had no idea. You want to stay at mine? Yeah, come and stay at mine. You can give...shit, sorry, I can't remember the name...'

'Marion.'

'Give Marion a call, try to sort things out.'

Roger looked down, swallowed hard.

'I don't want to do that. I want to stay there.'

'Where?'

'I want to stay at Goossens.'

'Are you fucking crazy? What you talking about?'

'I like it there. I want to stay there. That's why...' He stopped, lowered his voice to a whisper. 'That's why they can't knock it down.'

Spence sat back, gave Roger a quick up-and-down glance.

'I'm missing something here. Tell me what I'm missing here.'

'Nothing. I've told you...'

'You mean there's no angle?'

Roger blinked.

'You know people. You know everybody. You could get it stopped. The demolition.'

Spence frowned, then rubbed his forehead. 'Besides everything else about it, it happens to be a big ask. There'd have to be a good reason.'

Roger looked down, took a long breath. 'I'll show you.'

9

It was getting dark by the time they rolled on to the Composers', drawing looks at Spence's Mercedes, leather seats, automatic gearbox, alloy wheels.

'Nice car.' Roger had commented on getting in.

Spence rocked his head from side to side, suggesting ambivalence. 'Bored with it.' he said. 'Thinking of getting something a bit more sporty. Want to buy it? Do you a good deal.'

They travelled largely in silence from that point, Roger increasingly worried and Spence intrigued, eyes flashing at his uncomfortable passenger.

The smooth suspension dismissed another speed bump as Goossens came slowly into view over the other buildings.

'Home, sweet home.' commented Spence. 'Very comfy.'

Roger gave him instructions where to go. He leaped out in front of the gates and expertly opened the padlock with the key he'd copied from the collection Fitch had thrown him. Spence drove through into the secure spot, giving Roger a long look as he went by. He looked on with similar interest as Roger opened the access door and led him on to the service mezzanine.

'This is too weird.' he commented, looking upwards.

'Nothing to be afraid of.' said Roger as he started up the stairs, feeling suddenly more confident, generally happier to be back where he felt he belonged. Now that he'd brought Spence this far, he felt excited at the prospect of showing someone else his discovery, his new way of life.

'This brings back memories.' said Spence as he went slowly up the stairs behind him, crinkling his nose at the smell. 'Shitty memories, I might add.'

Roger had rushed up to the third floor while Spence dawdled, interested in something he saw from a small back window that faced over the canal.

'In here.' he called when he heard the scrape of Spence's shoes at the top of the steps on the third floor. Spence came in and looked around, taking the scene in, detail by detail.

Roger, in a cardigan he had just donned, stood awkwardly in the semicircular clearing he had made by pushing the rubbish back a few yards from the window side of the room. The armchair, draped in a giant pistachio bath towel, sat front and centre, commanding the prized view. Behind it on the floor lay a single inflatable bed with a pillow and an uncovered duvet. Some unironed clothes erupted from a duffel bag nearby and, on the other side of the armchair, a kettle stood next to an old coolbox and an array of plastic PoundBlaster bags.

Spence walked forward.

'This is it?' he asked.

Roger gestured towards the window and beyond. Spence got close to the edge and peered down, held by the vista for a few seconds. He looked back at Roger, who nodded towards the piazza.

'Just wait. It's starting to get dark. Hang on.'

He pulled his hands from within the pockets of the cardigan and rubbed the front of his thighs.

'Sorry, not being much of a host.' He looked down at the floor around him. 'Can I get you anything? Pot Noodle or a

CupaSoup or something?'

'Just ate, remember?'

'Of course. What am I thinking? How about a cup of tea.' he asked, squatting over the coolbox. 'Milk's fresh, I think.'

'Got anything stronger?'

'Yeah, sure. Beer?'

'Beer's fine.'

'Not all that cold.' he said, wrenching a can of PoundBlaster Pilsner from its plastic four-pack holder and throwing it across. Spence took a sip, made a face and turned back to the window. Roger stepped alongside him.

Their eyes were both caught by a standard group of adolescents who were circling at the back of the piazza, seven or eight, mostly male. It was difficult to make out clearly from this distance, but a small object was being handed around and brought up to the face for consumption. The general reaction was to stagger backwards and then bend double before handing it on. Each partaker was then emboldened to take their place inside an exiled supermarket trolley and be pushed at terrifying pace around the piazza until they collided with something. Or someone. One bystander, an elderly man walking his dog, was knocked to the ground and the lead caught behind one of the wheels. He was able to get up and hobble to the animal's aid just in time to save it from asphyxiation. However bone-shattering the collisions, the youths seemed always indestructible. When the first scooter cyclist of the evening appeared, parading himself like a peacock across the concrete, there was fierce discussion until the trolley was finally hooked up by a chain to the bike and pulled around the circumference road, the teenage girl inside shrieking for mercy until she reached an agreement with the driver, which meant their disappearance together into one of the dark garage entrances underneath Elgar. With their departure, the group fractured into smaller tribes.

Spence turned to Roger.

'Give me the keys.' he said.

Roger's heart sank.

'If you wait. The others will come out later. Then it's...'

'I want to get out. Just give me the keys.'

Roger handed them over and Spence walked out. Listening to the hurried steps as he descended the stairway, Roger slumped into the armchair. His eyelids felt heavy. He felt the ache in his shoulder returning as if a dimmer switch within was being turned up.

Spence was right, Roger tried telling himself. What was Roger, a grown man, doing here, surrounded by hydrogenated goods, watching morons perform wanton acts of destruction when he could be at home, with...his...family?

But it wasn't working. He wasn't convincing himself. He wanted to keep watching. Spence had been the last chance he had to save what he had here.

Looking on impassively as Spence's Merc emerged from underneath him and travelled smoothly around the perimeter of the piazza, he experienced a sensation of utter solitude. Spence, like his dad, like Marion, like everybody, had failed to understand what he was looking for, what he was trying to get away from, the beautiful simplicity he was trying to get close to.

And now about to be taken away. Razed to the ground.

He saw Spence's brake lights go on. Suddenly, the Mercedes mounted the kerb, near the corner where Pandy's Handy was situated. Roger watched as Spence got out, locked the car with a loud bleep, took one look directly up at the doomed Goossens and went into the shop. From where he was sitting, Roger could detect the almost imperceptible, instinctual drift of the piazza dwellers towards the alien presence, but too slow to be of any real threat. If Spence had just stopped to buy a packet of Hamlets, then he wouldn't have much more to contend with than a few cheeky demands for money.

But when Spence did emerge, a little later than Roger had anticipated, he was carrying what appeared to be four or five blue plastic bags stuffed full of purchases. Struggling with the weight, but apparently whistling, he waddled halfway across the piazza before placing all but one of them on a concrete bench with marked deliberation. Then, with a slightly more hurried gait, he headed back in Roger's direction.

When he heard the sound of the mezzanine-level door open, Roger rose and hurried to the doorway as a breathless Spence clambered up the steps and bustled past him.

'Got any clean glasses?' he asked.

Roger rooted in his effects and found a tube of disposable cups he'd nicked from the kitchen at work. He joined Spence right at the window just as the top was being spun off a bottle of Scotch.

'Only single malt he had in the whole shop.' complained Spence. 'Might be all right.'

He poured two glasses and they clinked polystyrene.

'Right.' said Spence, dialling a number on his mobile. 'Let's see if that gets things going a bit.'

'What did you leave on the bench?' Roger asked.

'Cider and vodka to get them pissed. And Red Blast to get them wired. See if it works.' said Spence, listening for a ringing tone.

'What about your car?'

Spence sniffed. 'That's how we'll know if it's worked.' Someone came on the line. 'Hello.' he said. 'I'd like to report a stolen vehicle.' He cupped the mouthpiece to speak to Roger. 'Like I said, fancy a new one anyway.'

It took about ten minutes before the first inspection of the bags was made, then a further three before the first fight broke out over its control. The signs were promising when, within the half-hour, the entire pack were using the supermarket trolley in a ramraid on Pandy's store, a couple inside it using metal bars like medieval lances as they were propelled towards the reinforced glass. But only when the collective attention was finally directed towards Spence's car, when each window was systematically smashed, each tyre slashed, the roof and bonnet crushed underfoot, fireworks set off into the exhaust and out through the sunroof, only when the miracle of German engineering was fully ablaze was Spence prepared to declare his cocktail a success.

'Ha! Excellent. What do you think of that?'

Roger could only smile.

'Barmy.' added Spence. 'Absolute headers, the lot of them.'

'I envy them.' Roger said quietly. 'Their freedom. I envy it.'

Spence took a quick shot of the whisky, smacked his lips together.

'You know what?'

Roger looked across to find out.

'I'm thinking.' Spence said. 'I'm thinking people would pay money to see this.'

He slapped Roger on the shoulder, a laugh in his eyes.

'*Good* money. You're right, old son. This demolition's a no-no. Not with a business opportunity like this staring us right in the mush.'

10

Spence talked excitedly about the project but Roger wasn't really paying attention, preferring to savour each sip of whisky and listen to the lapping of the water around them as the oars slid down and up from the surface. A warm satisfaction rendered him pleasantly sleepy; partly the single malt but also the happiness at having Spence on board with him, at the feeling of companionship as they drifted down the dark corridor together.

'Keep that bloody torch up.' Spence told him. 'I'm close to the bank here.'

Roger raised the beam that he had allowed to let slip and could see that Spence was right. The silty edge of the canal was only a few feet away. Spence began favouring one oar to propel them back towards the middle of the water.

The torch was essential for it was surprisingly dark. Roger wasn't sure what the time was but guessed it was around 2 a.m. They had watched 'the Show', as Spence had quickly dubbed it, for a few hours. It was an average evening's fun, with its highlight a memorable catfight between two middle-aged women over the ownership of what looked like a large felt jester's hat. The stamping and gouging were watched by an appreciative crowd until an honourable draw was declared and the hat was ceremonially burned on the embers of Spence's car, the gladiatrixes comparing wounds over Bacardi Breezers. Not long after, a light but persistent drizzle sent most of the troupe indoors. Only a few gaunt, hooded souls with limited control of their limbs remained when Spence had yawned and stretched.

'I reckon that'll do it for tonight.'

Roger looked upwards to the sky, saw the rain getting heavier as it flashed by a streetlight.

'Might stop in a minute.' he ventured, but Spence was already standing to go.

'Nah.' he said. 'Anyway, need to get some sleep. We get cracking tomorrow, sack the demolition, then start on this place.'

Roger looked around. 'Start on what?'

'Clear it up. Lick of paint, I don't know. We're going to have paying guests, we'll have to do something. Shouldn't be too hard. There.' he went on, framing the shuttered canteen with two outstretched hands. 'You've got your bar area already. Few settees over here, then we set up a little stand of seats. People can come and go, watch the action. Mind you.' he added, talking to himself now. 'If it rains and we're washed out, have to give them their money back, I suppose...' He extracted himself from the thought. 'Come on, let's go.'

Roger stood still, a question in his eyes.

'You can stay at mine.' answered Spence. 'I've got a futon in the spare room. And I need your help getting out of here.'

'I was wondering about that.' Roger said, looking down. However unorganised they were now, nothing would unite the half a dozen or so still on the piazza more than the sight of two pedestrians trying to pass through them. 'You car's not...' he reminded Spence.

But Spence tapped the side of his head. 'Way ahead of you.' he said and headed for the stairs. 'Bring the torch.

And the booze.'

He'd spotted the rowing boat from the window on the staircase on the way up, half-hidden among the dense foliage that had grown unchecked for years. The presence of two oars was down to luck, but Roger had always considered Spence to be lucky in a way that he had never been. Even so, extracting the boat and dragging it down to the water's edge took a lot of effort. Roger felt his back tacky with sweat as he clambered in and sat at the stern as Spence planted the wrong end of an oar into the bank and pushed them into the canal.

As they moved gently along its course, Roger was impressed by the speed of Spence's thought but found the detail difficult to follow. That didn't matter. What mattered, what he was sure of, was that Goossens would stand. The good thing he'd found wouldn't be lost, even though that meant sharing it with more others than he might have liked. He was prepared to make compromises.

One question clouded his mind. He wanted to ask it but Spence interrupted him.

'There.' he said, nodding as they came around a bend to a clearing on the opposite side of the canal, lit from above in a jaundiced haze by two sodium streetlamps.

'What's that?' Roger asked.

'Jetty.' groaned Spence, pulling hard to steer the boat across. 'Used to drop off coal for the old steel mill here. It's only about half a mile to the coast road. We'll pick up a cab from there.'

Together they pulled the boat up on to the mottled concrete of the small dock and hid it behind a large horizontal gas cylinder before setting off down the path. The detail that had been nagging at Roger came back.

'One thing.' he said. 'How are we going to get punters in and out without drawing attention to the fact that they're piling into a derelict building?'

Spence stopped in his tracks and shone the torch in his face.

'Come on, Rodge, old son. What have we just been doing for the last hour?'

Roger shrugged. 'Rowing down the…' he said, slowing down as the penny dropped.

'Canal.' they said in unison.

'Ah.' Roger exhaled, stepping off to follow Spence's brisk pace.

'They arrive here by car, we collect them here, twenty minutes down the water, drinks on board obviously, switch off the engines as we approach, bring them in through the back. Take them home the same way. Piece of piss.'

Spence marched on but Roger had to stop again for a moment and look back at the jetty, almost out of view now.

'Engines?' he muttered, then ran to catch up.

PART TWO

11

Spence's insurance company had come up with a courtesy car by half-nine the next morning. Roger was up and well rested a half-hour later, sitting at the breakfast bar in Spence's spacious kitchen with a bacon sandwich and a cup of coffee from his expensive-looking espresso machine. He couldn't dismiss the sense of dreamy wellbeing from the night before as the sound of Spence's businesslike baritone drifted through from the sitting room at the front of the house. Roger couldn't pick up the words but the words didn't matter as much as the tone, direct and confident. Spence was pulling the right strings, pressing the right buttons. When he came through to the kitchen a few minutes later he was dragging his coat on.

'Come on.' he told Roger, who slurped down the last of his coffee.

'Where we going?'

'Where do you think?' said Spence, picking up his new car keys and shoving them into his pocket. 'We're going to work. What are you supposed to be doing today?'

Work. In the company of Spence, whose full-time employment was little more than a sideline, Roger had forgotten about work. 'Er, nothing special. Whatever.'

'Good. Let's go.'

In the car Spence, struggling to familiarise himself with the new dashboard, updated Roger on his progress.

'Right, good news and bad news on the demolition.'

'Yeah?'

'There's a long-term solution.' said Spence on an out-breath. 'Where's the indicators on this fucking thing…? The demolition is practical as long as the numbers on the Composers' don't get any bigger. If the population goes over a certain level, then health and safety regs would mean they'd have to take it down brick by brick, which is too expensive.'

'Great. So what do we do?'

Spence stuck out his bottom lip as they stopped at traffic lights and shook the gear stick from side to side. 'We get more bodies on the Composers'. The right sort. Proper head-bangers. DemoRent won't put up a fuss. They're only taking it on to try to shore up the long-term contract. They're happier blowing up listed cottages.'

Roger shook his head. 'But Housing aren't locating tenants to the Composers' any more. Not since that thing.'

'What thing?'

'The thing. The thing…with the meths drinker and the indoor barbecue.'

Spence puffed out his cheeks, shook his head in recollection.

'Besides which.' Roger went on, 'most of the flats people are living in are barely habitable. Christ knows what the empty ones are like.'

'Fair point. That's why we need to get Housing on board.'

Roger looked across. Spence was ready for him.

'Look, Rodge, I know this is your baby, I know it's a personal thing for you, but you have to face facts. If we're going to make a go of this, we have to let other people in on it. This is going to take organisation. We couldn't keep this a total secret, even if we wanted to.'

'So what are you suggesting?' asked Roger, sighing.

'I get a few of the Housing boys in to see what we've got. Three or four of them working on it should be enough. I know the right ones. They'll be well up for it. They can give the bodgers a green light to get enough flats up to minimum standard and then we bus in a load of chavs to smash them up again. But they're not going to do it unless they're in the loop.' He glanced over at Roger. 'I can't see any other way of doing it.'

Roger felt a hollowness inside. The sharing of his dark pleasure was not what he had wanted. Perhaps he'd been naive to think that it could go no further than Spence, but the idea, ventured within hours, of untold numbers traipsing through his sanctuary on the third floor left him heavy-eyed.

Spence clocked his mood. Uncharacteristically, he stopped at a pelican crossing to let a senior citizen hobble across the road on a pair of sticks. It gave him the time to tug on the handbrake and lean across.

'Rodge, it's up to you. You came to me and I'm giving you the score. I can do this, we can do this. Everyone who comes in on it will know where you stand, that it's your finder's fee…We get the right people, ones we can trust, this could be a serious goer. I can feel it. It's going to be…' He stopped and sniggered at the thought of it. 'Here's your choice. You can spend the next five years running ASBOs on these shitkickers or we can put them to work for our benefit. Those idiots trashing up their own neighbourhood and us getting rich on the back of it. Pease out of the loop. I fucking love it.'

Roger couldn't help but find Spence's enthusiasm infectious. 'Rich?'

Spence shrugged. 'Who knows? But if you don't want to go ahead with it, just tell me now. Say the word and we call it off.'

There it was. An implicit challenge. Spence was a master of these situations, an arch negotiator. Roger was unable to think of anything except what his father would do. Which left him no choice.

'No, we're going ahead.'

'Attaboy.'

Spence dropped the handbrake, shunted the car into gear and swerved around the pensioner, who'd stopped in the middle of the road for a breather.

Roger drew himself higher in his seat, felt a sudden surge of adrenalin at his new decisiveness. 'So, what's first?'

'Like I said, that was the good news. It's going to take a few weeks to get things sorted out, get the renovations done. The demolition could still happen in the meantime.' He put up a hand to cut Roger off at the pass. 'Don't worry. We just need a stopgap measure in the meantime. When we get to the office, I want you to go up to the fourth floor and pop into the Gypsy Love Machine. I can't go. I'm not liked up there.'

'Eh?' asked Roger. 'Why me?' He didn't think he'd get any warmer a welcome in the grotto of rectitudinous thinking that was the council's Traveller Liaison Unit, where an effigy of Fitch hung from a noose on the back of the door.

'They'll smell a rat if it was me.'

'What am I going there for?'

'Simple. Pikeys. We want to know who the smelliest ones are and we want to know where to find them. Then we're going to offer them a hundred quid a family to move underneath Goebbels.' Spence swung the steering wheel hard with one hand. 'It's ironic, isn't it?' he commented. 'Exactly the people who should have a building dropped on them are going to be the ones to stop it happening.'

Roger laughed. Spence reached in his top pocket and pulled out his mobile phone, brought it up to eye level, his thumb performing gymnastics across the keypad.

'In the meantime.' he said, putting it to his ear. 'Mate? It's me. How's it going? Everything all right with that delivery?

Sweet, mate. Glad to hear it…What's that?…Fucking right…In your dreams, son…No, listen. I've got a job for you. Funsize, mate, you are going to love this. This is the ultimate challenge. I want you to get me…Wait for it…I want you to find me…a canal boat.'

It took forty-five minutes for Funsize to call back, as Spence and Roger were walking through the city centre.

'Excellent.' said Spence, after he hung up. 'He's found us one moored next to the site of a freight company that went bust a few months ago. Looks like the family have fucked off to Spain for good. Nobody's going to miss it. Another piece of the jigsaw clicks into place.'

As usual, Roger was having to hurry to keep up as Spence took a left down the side of the Central Library, heading towards the subways that went underneath the dual carriageway at its back.

'How are we going to move a barge? I've never even been on a barge.'

'No? I went on holiday to the Broads once. Pissed down the whole time. Sacked it after a day and a half.'

'And that qualifies you?'

'Fucking hell.' said Spence, puffing out his cheeks as they descended into the poorly lit subway, the echoes of their footsteps snapping around them. 'Never let it be said that I don't know my own limitations. No, we need an expert, someone who's comfortable on the water. An old salty sea dog. There he is, over there.'

Roger peered forward to a low figure, who was in a sitting position against the wall, knees peeping through a large, scrofulous greatcoat. A laminated cardboard badge bearing a photograph and a number hung from a piece of plastic twine that emerged from an unruly beard. A pile of damp, dog-eared magazines lay before him to which he silently gestured.

'Why would I want to read that shit?' asked Spence, gesturing around him. 'And this is a stupid bloody place to set up, isn't it? Who ever comes down here?'

The man flexed his shoulders. 'It's my spot.' Roger detected the edge of an Irish brogue.

'Well, you're the worst fucking *Big Issue* seller I've ever seen. And that's saying something.'

The man stuck out an arm, which Spence seized and pulled him up by. At his full height he was an imposing figure. Roger thought he might know this bloke.

'I'll admit.' he said, straightening out his coat, 'it's not my vacation.'

Spence laughed. '*Vo*cation. But don't worry. I've got something much more up your street. How would you like to get back on the water, Norman?'

Roger opened his mouth in delayed recognition. He and Spence walked out of the tunnel, led at a brisk naval step by none other than Goossens' last-ever concierge.

12

SIX DAYS LATER

Roger was up on the third floor, making tea in the corner canteen with a slight headache from the noise of the radio that hadn't been quite tuned in to Civic for the last two hours. Outside, it was a bright afternoon, the sun glaring through the newly cleaned window, making visibility a little difficult for the council painters, a few of whom were putting the finishing touches to a second coat on the walls as the rest tidied up. Cleared of rubbish, the room looked twice as big as it had before, a truly commanding space. Looking down through the window, beyond the banks of chairs 'borrowed' from one of the council's forgotten meeting rooms, he could just make out the edge of the gypsy encampment as it spilled over the perimeter of the piazza. It had been less than a week since he'd popped up to Traveller Liaison with his innocent enquiry. Now they had half the pikeys in the municipal borough camped under Goossens' shadow, including a number who'd turned up with no financial motive. News of the trouble that had been flaring up between their fellow itinerants and the incumbent population of the Composers' had been incentive

enough. The instinctual hostility had escalated from initial suspicion to the brink of violence, providing some fine
entertainment for Roger, Spence and the boys from Housing.
They'd come down at the start of the week in an obvious
mood of scepticism but had returned every night since then,
just lapping it up. They'd also been generous with their dope,
for which Roger had surprised himself by developing a defi-
nite penchant. Roger found that it helped tone down his
general anxiety at watching the Show becoming a common
property. Last night, during a slight lull when the police had
unsportingly tried to ease the tension down on the piazza,
Darren from Housing had tutored Roger in how to roll his first
spliff. Now he stood, drying cups and occasionally patting his
pocket where the small cube of cannabis resin Darren had
given him rested. He wondered when he might get a chance
to sit down for half an hour and skin up in peace and quiet.

He was distracted by the sound of the industrial-sized tea
urn, its 'council property' sticker inexpertly ripped off, clicking
and the red light at its base coming on, the sign that the gallons of water inside had boiled. He flipped the lid on the first
of the giant metal teapots the boys from Property Renovation
had brought with them and opened the urn tap to fill it.

'Tea!' he shouted.

The fifteen of them, virtually the entire complement of
council-paid decorators, downed brushes. Roger had been
concerned that using virtually everybody on the books might
draw attention to what they were doing but Spence had been
unperturbed.

'We need it done by tonight. And anyway, it's Friday.
Nobody worries where they are on a Friday.'

Roger started pouring and handing mugs over the counter,
letting the overalled workers put in their own astonishing
number of sugars. Despite what Spence had assured him,
Roger didn't get the feeling that they understood who he was,

how he fitted in to the scheme of things. He was just the guy making the tea.

As if to emphasise the point, the atmosphere changed as Spence himself came clopping up the stairs and on to the third floor and the general attention was redirected towards him.

'All right, boys?' he wanted to know, stopping to inspect the progress. 'Looking good.' he commented, reaching into his back pocket. 'Suppose you'll want paying?'

He produced a thick roll of notes and held it up. The group advanced towards him but he waved his wad with a note of warning.

'Now, remember. Payment is made on the agreement that you talk about this job to nobody. And you all take the barge back, understood?' He waved his wad. 'There's going to be plenty more where this came from, but if any of you coughs, I'll find out who you are and you'll end up cleaning public gents at witching hour. Although.' he said, picking one of them out, 'you might quite fancy that, Parkesy.'

The laughter was relaxed. Roger realised he was only restating an axiomatic condition of service. They'd all done this kind of thing before, he presumed as they formed an orderly queue and Spence began sliding fifties off the top of his bundle and handing them out, three at a time.

When he'd finished, Spence headed towards the canteen. Roger slid a mug towards him across the counter top.

'Ready for the big night, mein host?' Spence asked, widening his eyes and giving a little shiver.

'Suppose.'

'Come on, Rodge, let's see a bit more enthusiasm. We're in business here.' He gestured towards the piazza. 'It's not as if it's a hard sell. Chavs v. Gyppos. One fall, one submission or a knockout. I've just been talking to Pandy. He reckons it's going to kick off for real tonight. Perfect timing.' he said, rubbing his hands together then glancing down at the boxes of PoundBlaster Cava lying next to the fridge. 'That the booze?'

Roger nodded.

'All right. We need that unpacked, get the sparkly in the fridge. Beer's on its way. Fucking catering services have come up short with the glasses, so we'll have to use plastic cups tonight.' He took a gulp of tea then remembered something. 'Oh yeah, I got a couple of girls from the staff canteen to come and serve the drinks. Little black dresses, I told them. They'll be good. Like a party, those two. Hey, by the way, have you checked out upstairs?'

'Yeah.'

'What do you think?'

'Yeah. I like it.'

'Place of your own. We get a bit more furniture in it, you'll be set up. I've arranged to get you a proper bed. That nursing home up on Stokes Hill, they've had to cut back on residents. It's one of those ones you can sit up in, good for reading in bed.'

'Great. Cheers.'

Spence had another look around. 'Right. I'm going to go down and pay Norman his wages. You want to come down, see what he's done to the boat. Bloody amazing.'

Roger hadn't seen the boat since the day it had been dragged in by a tug over a week ago, and he had assumed that their grand plan had faltered at the first hurdle. It had been a grim sight, covered in a nasty grime of oil and soot with a grinding cough brought on by any attempt to turn over its engine. Seeing it now, nestling on the water out of sight around the back of Goossens House, its motor running as smoothly as a dialling tone and the colourful markings that had always been there lovingly revealed, Roger could hardly credit that it was the same vehicle.

'Ahoy.' shouted Spence. 'Cap'n Birdseye!'

Norman's head and giant shoulders appeared from a hole in the decking. He clocked them both with his usual mad stare, no less mad since he'd had his hair cut and his facial hair trimmed at Spence's expense.

'It's you.' he commented, planting both hands on the deck and hauling himself up. 'Just doing some work on the sump.' he added, eyeing them closely.

Roger nodded. 'Looks great.' he said.

'Managed to find her true self underneath all that shite.' Norman said, rubbing his hands with a rag. 'Bit like myself, you might say.' He scanned the length of the vessel, snorted hard. 'Built by Yarwood, late 1930s.'

'Was he good?'

Norman nodded. 'Craftsman. Simple narrowboat construction, with your Widdop single-cylinder diesel running her. Twenty-odd horsepower. Slow and steady, like me good self.'

'Looks like she's got some history.'

'You'd be right about that. Would have been built for carrying grain, I reckon, then switched to coal later. I like her.' he added. 'I like her personality.'

Spence scoffed. 'A barge is a barge, isn't it?' he said, rummaging for his mobile as it bleeped the receipt of a text message.

'Away wi'cha and your fucking blasphemy.' roared Norman. 'There are as many types of river boat as there are ways for me to kill you with my bare hands.'

'And how many's that?' smiled Spence, starting to punch a reply into his phone.

'Fucking plenty. So watch what you say around her. I grew up with boats like her. Used to watch the Guinness heading out down the Grand Canal on the *Killiney* as a boy…'

Spence laughed out loud. 'You're making that up. Spare us

the leprechaun bollocks.'

Norman gave Spence one of his inscrutable stares for a moment, then shook his head. 'Think what you like. I know what I seen. Simpler life in them days.' he mused, picking up a copy of the *Argus* and rapping the front page with a full set of knuckles. 'Better times. Not like this shite.'

He held it up to show them the leading story.

MONSTER RELEASED, it read. Roger had seen it already. Victor Bronsky, the alleged child-abuser, had walked after the judge had said a fair trial was impossible following biased press coverage and countless unruly interventions from the public gallery. Despite his new-found freedom, the police had had to use three decoy vans alongside the one he actually left in to get Bronsky past the baying hordes outside. Spence didn't show a lot of interest aside from raising an eyebrow. Roger shook his head ruefully.

'Guy's entitled to a fair trial.'

Norman didn't agree. 'So it's all right to have yer fucking paedophiles—' he stretched out the long *e* of 'paedophile' for an eternity '—roaming the streets now, is it?'

'Not saying it's right. Just saying that's the system. Innocent until proven guilty.'

'Unless we're slapping an ASBO on you, when we can heap shit on you for something you haven't done yet.' chipped in Spence mischievously.

'People can't control themselves.' Roger went on, ignoring him 'That's how it comes down.'

'Not right.' said Norman, rubbing his hand across the grain at the top of the gunwale. 'Place is crawling with *peeeeeeeed*-ophiles and yer fecking hormone-sensuals.'

'I wouldn't worry.' Spence added, slipping the phone back in his pocket with obvious self-satisfaction at something. 'The charvies have their own justice system. They'll run him down and string him up. It's in the natural order of things.' He checked his watch. 'First party's going to be here in an hour. Let's get shipshape, me hearties.'

Roger and Spence stood on the concrete jetty, not saying much. Both looked up as the twin sodium lamps came on above them, barely making inroads into the gathering gloom. Roger offered Spence a toke on his spliff but it was declined, Spence preferring to bob from one foot to the other, a motion that irritated Roger as much as the swarm of midges that danced above the lapping water between the jetty and the barge.

Roger put the cigarette to his mouth and bit hard on the roach, sucking the smoke tightly through his teeth. He would have preferred to be on the barge with Norman, trying to let a little of the Irishman's studied lack of interest rub off on him. But Spence, ever keen to keep Roger involved, had insisted they wait together on the jetty. Now, when push was coming to shove, Roger actually wanted to take a back seat. He wasn't so comfortable being heralded as the discoverer of new territories any more.

It had been Spence's idea for them to dress up as well. Having to wear a shirt and tie made Roger feel uncomfortable and brought back the beginning of the ache in his shoulder.

'So who's coming?' Roger asked, admittedly late in the day.

'Friends. Contacts. Council people, mainly. I thought we'd spread our net narrow to start with.'

Roger nodded and blew the smoke out, Spence taking a step to the side to avoid being caught in the cloud.

'Hasn't taken you long to turn into a hophead.' he commented.

'It's medicinal.'

'Yeah, well, don't forget to offer it around, if that's what they want. I've trailed this as a party, remember.'

'Not really in a party mood.'

'Well, you'd better get into one, pronto.' he said, turning towards two points of light that were moving erratically towards them. 'We're on.'

The first cars bounced down the potholed road towards them, the drivers sweeping wide as they met the jetty and drawing up right next to where Spence stood.

The doors opened and out poured five people, four men and a woman. Roger knew a couple by name, recognised the others from his long constitutionals down the council corridors.

'So what's going on, Spence?' one of them asked, stretching and yawning.

'All in good time, Barry.' said Spence. 'You're the first lot to get here.'

'What you selling this time?' asked Graham Figg from Tendering. 'If it's any more of them cemetery plots, you can count me out. I'm getting cremated.'

'Sell you a match, then.' Spence came straight back.

'I'm skint.' declared the female among them, who Roger thought worked in the Parks Department. 'And I've still got three cases of that Jacob's Creek you nicked off the mayor in my garage.'

Spence laughed. 'For me to have nicked it, he'd have to have seen it in the first place.'

All out of the car, they looked around.

'So what we up to?' asked Graham. 'Seriously.'

'Heard you been busy.' said the woman. 'Gypsy Love Machine's not happy about something.'

'Can't find a decorator for love nor money.' added the one called Barry.

Spence held out a hand. 'All in good time, all in good time. But first.' he continued, planting a hand on Roger's back and pushing him forward. 'Some of you already know Roger…'

He was introduced and shook hands, only then realising

how grubby his fingernails were.

'Roger is the brains behind the operation. I've been able to sort a few things out but he's the guy who deserves all the credit. Now—' he pointed to the barge '—if you'd care to board our bespoke conveyance, where we've got drinks laid on for you, we'll be leaving in a few minutes to show you something I think you're going to enjoy…'

They waited for one more carload to arrive before the journey began, Spence passing the ten minutes with a little speech about how select the group on this boat were, then adding an exhortation for everyone to enjoy themselves. If they liked what they saw tonight, then feel free to pass the word around to people who can be trusted to retain a degree of circumspection. If the wrong people, by whom he meant the Old Bill, or most (but not all) of the local council committee, got wind, then the operation would cease.

'But I'm sitting here.' he rounded off, 'absolutely positive that each and every one of you will want to come back to see more of what we have to offer. I have only one final request. In a few moments, the engines will be turned off. It's important that you all remain as quiet as possible from that period until you enter the building you'll be shown into. I can't stress how important that is. Absolute silence.'

Roger listened admiringly to Spence's expert patter, seeing in it the secret of his friend's success. Sitting on the set of steps that led down into the cabin, he marvelled at how complete Spence's preparation had been in such a short space of time. You massage their egos enough, then you can make them do anything. They couldn't see they were being used. If they wanted to come again, they'd have to fork out the fifty quid like everybody else. And pay for their own drinks.

A few moments later, the churning of the engines cut out.

'All stop!' cried Norman, pointlessly, from the bow.

Spence smarted and hissed at Roger: 'Can you fucking tell

him *not* to do that!'

Looks were exchanged among the invitees as the narrow-boat went into drift down the channel. But Norman, as he had done on several runs transporting people and equipment over the last few days, steered the last half-mile expertly towards the rows of old tyres, connected with rope, that sat in the water as a soft docking station right alongside Goossens. Roger now recognised the sound of the small ramp being attached to the side of the canal.

Spence pushed his fingers to his lips one last time and nodded for Roger to open the hatch. Good as gold, they filed through, across the bank, through the small door. Nearing the summit, he found the invited assembly congregating at the top of the stairs. Spence had run on ahead and it was his voice that encouraged them to follow him through.

'Come on, ladies and gentlemen.'

Roger followed them into the low-lit room. The smell of fresh paint still hung heavy. Away to the right, four sofas were laid out in a square, facing each other over a large glass coffee table. Two slim girls stood enticingly behind the bar, flutes and champagne buckets set out before them. And in front of the window, two banks of seats, the back row raised on a semicircular plinth, awaited occupation.

'Emily and Joss will serve you with drinks. If you'd like to just make yourself comfortable. And whenever you're ready.' he added, sweeping his arm out towards the piazza, where Roger thought he could see a gypsy caravan on fire and one prone figure protecting his head from a shower of kicks nearby, 'feel free to take in the best floorshow in town.'

Barely able to take their eyes off it, they moved forward, stumbling over their chairs.

13

FIVE WEEKS LATER

Roger sat in the office with the same feeling of uneasiness he'd had for a while still haunting him. Despite its familiarity in so many other ways, he still found it strange to be in a place where everyone wasn't talking about the Show, when it had dominated his life to such an extent for the last month or more. A few feet away, Mason sat, making some new entry in his genealogical diagram of ratbags, chatting away in what was basically a monologue about his favourite subject.

'…what I'm saying is they're very skilled in pushing the envelope, you know what I mean?' he said, running a long ruler line from one corner of the page to the other. 'They understand what the taboos are and they go as close as you can get. I mean.' he went on, gesturing down at his handiwork, 'to shack up with your own stepbrother's half-sister, that's got to feel like incest even if it isn't.'

'Sounds exactly like what the aristocracy get up to.' said a somnolent Dennis Priest, massaging the bridge of his nose with both index fingers.

'Yeah, but with the aristocracy it's business. They're practical about it. Our friends here haven't got dowries or land rights.'

'Maybe they're in love.' piped up Maxine.

Mason smirked. 'Maybe. But then why advertise it? He's shagging her from behind over the balcony railing where everyone can see, waving to people going by. There's a perfectly good bedroom a few yards away. Everybody has to get an eyeful. The point is that they're brazen about it. They want to invoke some outrage and then rub people's noses in it. They want people to watch.'

Roger looked up at him, caught his eye.

'What?' asked Mason with a small laugh, suggesting he was slightly unnerved.

He didn't know. Couldn't know. *Could he?*

'Nothing.' said Roger, tugging at his eyelid.

His new mobile phone, its ringing tone turned off, buzzed violently on the desk in front of him. He picked it up to take the call.

'Hello…yes.' he admitted, eyes dancing around the room conspiratorially and lowering his voice. 'What night you after?…Wait a minute. I'll have to check.'

He quickly unlocked the drawer in his desk and took out the page-a-day diary he'd nicked from stationery, leafed through the well-used pages for recent dates until reaching a week on Saturday, screwing up his face and whispering into the phone.

'Sorry, but we're pretty much booked up for the Saturday…Just a sec…No, the next two Saturdays are pretty jammed as well…I know, but it's just a question of how many people we can physically transport over. If it was one or two of you, that might be different, but groups of double figures…'
He puffed out his cheeks. 'There isn't much until the middle of next month…OK, just the two of you then. OK, that

should be fine…Have you got a membership number?…OK, then, if I can have your name and details…'

As he started writing, Spence bustled in, wearing a long, expensive-looking wool overcoat, cashmere scarf wrapped loosely around his neck and carrying a cardboard box which he dropped heavily on his otherwise clear desk.

'All right, everyone?' he wanted to know in an unfamiliar blast of cheeriness before making straight for Roger's desk, pulling up a stray chair and sitting down.

'You get that money?' he asked.

'Yeah. Thanks.'

'Don't thank me.' said Spence, pulling up the lapels on his coat. 'Thank the artistes.'

There was something in his behaviour that almost seemed calculated to suggest conspiracy, Roger thought, as if he deliberately wanted to incite curiosity among the others. Roger was aware of Mason surreptitiously watching them, wanting to know what they were discussing.

'There was a bit of a rumpus after you went to bed.'

Roger shook his head.

'Didn't hear anything from upstairs.' Not surprising when he'd been wearing headphones and watching CostBlast on his newly installed cable service, watching Lorraine sporting an ankle bracelet, an erection in one hand and a spliff in the other.

'Yeah. Nothing major. Drink got spilled. Handbags, really. But it got me thinking about security. Just to keep a lid on things. Especially after what happened on Friday.'

Roger nodded. On Friday they'd had their first unexpected clients, two pissheads from the agricultural college who'd canoed down the canal to find them. They'd been let in for their cheek but Spence and Roger knew it wasn't a good precedent.

'If you think…' agreed Roger. 'Who've you got in mind?'

Spence smirked, widened his eyes. 'Who's the last person you would mess with?'

They both looked across at Maxine just as she looked up from her desk, holding up a small mirror to reinforce her pink lipstick.

'What you twats looking at?' she wanted to know.

'Just the future of law enforcement.' said Spence. He tapped his watch and made a drinking motion towards her, then pointed to Mason and did the same.

'What you asking him for?' Roger asked, mildly panicked.

'Something else I've been thinking about. Bookings going OK?'

'Yeah. Good. Very good.'

'Lot of repeat visitors, yeah?'

'Yeah.'

Spence nodded, his thinking confirmed. 'People are going to keep coming back. They'll be OK the first two or three times. The novelty factor, right? But we have to find a way to make them keep coming after that. I thought it would help if people could identify different characters on the piazza, ones to look out for. They're going to have their favourites. You know, like the wrestling.'

Roger cocked his head. He got the idea.

'But we'd need a spotter.' said Spence, warming to his theme, giving Roger the medium-hard sell, 'someone who can tell one chav from another, someone who knows a bit about each of them…an expert on the subject.'

'Mason?' said Roger, folding his arms.

'Mason. Look, it'll make life easier, anyway. If they're onside, they can cover for us when we're out on Show business. It's better than trying to keep it a secret.'

'The more people who know…you'll be getting Dennis in on it next.'

'Great idea. I'll pop in and see Pease as well. He can stuff the vol-au-vents.'

He spread out his palms, asking for Roger's blessing, which he gave with a blink and a shrug.

'Good call.' said Spence, suddenly remembering something. 'Here, I almost forgot. Got a call earlier. Tonight—' he paused for effect '—we are moving into media circles.'

'Who?'

'Tell you later.' he said, nodding across to where Fitch had just emerged from his office, waving a fax, curled up at the edges.

'Has anyone seen this?' he asked, planting one hand on his hip and bringing the paper to his forehead. 'This takes the fucking biscuit. Get this.'

'What's up, boss?' asked Spence.

'Housing are only going and fucking relocating to the Composers'.'

'You're joking.' Mason splurted a laugh.

Fitch was incandescent but he tried to restrain himself as he referred to the offending document. '"Policy review. Redevelopment of existing housing stock on Composers' Estate and relocation of existing tenants including…including fucking ASBO recipients." They actually make a point of saying that. It's just…it's beyond fucking belief! We try to put a stop to these fucking scags while our right hand is rewarding them with brand-new fucking apartments in Dodge City. It's as if—' He screwed the paper up and threw it at the door of his own office, spinning himself around on his heels '—we've got virtually no control there as it is. You would honestly think …you would actually think that they were deliberately going out of their way to create a sink estate. They're doing this to spite me. I know it.'

Spence puffed out his cheeks and shook his head.

'Don't take it personally, guv.'

'Maybe I should take this straight to Pease.' said Fitch,

thinking out loud. 'Cut out the hempshaggers and take it straight upstairs.'

Spence stood up a little too quickly, brushed a hand down his coat. 'You don't want to do that.' he said, the tip of his tongue creeping out from the corner of his mouth. 'This'll have gone through him already.' he improvised. 'Everything does now. Anyway, it smacks of him. It's tight-fisted, isn't it, bodging up old stock?'

'More bloody expensive in the long run.' complained Fitch but with the hint of defeat in his voice. He picked up the crushed memo and began to unfurl it. 'I mean, just look at this…' He searched for the passage he wanted, quickly opening and closing his mouth like a fish until he found it. 'Here we go, dah dah dah… "As a result of proposed relocations, Health & Safety have notified that all scheduled demolitions on this site are now under review." Classic short-termism. That means Goebbels stays up. Now they've got maintenance costs year in, year out on a derelict deathtrap. It's just…ah.'

'Come on.' said Spence, 'you've worked for the council long enough. Don't tell me you're surprised.'

Fitch's shoulders sagged. 'You're right.' he confessed. 'There's no point in kicking up about it. I shouldn't be. But…' He tried to start again but was too exhausted. 'One thing I can do.' he said, calmer. 'I'm keeping you lot away from the Composers'.'

'Ah.' moaned Mason. 'But it's going to kick off massively. The craic'll be huge.'

But Fitch shook his head.

'They want a fucking no-go area, they can have one. Everyone they're moving in is going to be ASBOed up already. I'm not sanctioning any visits down there without serious police presence. End of story.' he finished off, reaching the threshold of his office.

'By the way, boss,' Spence called. 'Did you get that e-mail I sent you?'

Fitch raised his eyebrows, stared into space. 'E-mail?'

'I asked if it was OK to use a couple of days down at the magistrates' court, check out the ASBO procedures down there. I thought I might do a report on it, see if we could streamline procedures on the back of it.'

Fitch's mind was still elsewhere. 'Yeah, that should be fine.'

'Roger says he fancies coming along. Would that be all right?'

Roger glanced from side to side. First he knew about it. But his surprise was lost on Fitch, who'd turned his back and given a perfunctory wave in the positive.

Spence sat down and clapped Roger on the shoulder.

'How about that? Result.' he said, loud enough for every-one to hear. 'We're in business. So.' he said to Mason, 'you fancy it down on the Composers' then?'

Mason dropped his biro on the desk. 'What, with every charvie headbanger living on top of each other? Fuck, I'd be well up for it. Wouldn't want to live there, mind. But you heard what he said.'

Spence just smiled at him, making Mason furrow his brow in curiosity. Spence's teasing pantomime was making Roger feel uncomfortable. With the brick of fifties Spence had given him as his share of the profits so far clogging his wallet, he wasn't complaining about how things had panned out. But however pleased he was with the new revelation that Goossens had been effectively spared, in his heart he felt that too many people knew already. Spence clocked his mood as they went out into the corridor to get coffee.

'Come on, Rodge.' he whispered, biting his lip and giving him a gentle punch on the shoulder. 'We're having fun, aren't we?'

Roger nodded but he knew what the problem was. The

Show wasn't about fun for him. It was altogether more serious. He feared, genuinely feared, that nobody else really understood that. This feeling of isolation was making him tense, he realised. He'd have to go and see Darren. His cannabis supply was dwindling. He needed to keep calm. That was paramount.

He shook off the thought in favour of another one that was troubling him.

'Anyway, what was all that about the magistrates' court?'

'Research. Like I said.'

'Be serious.'

'I am.' Spence insisted, looking around. 'Now Housing have got the green light on relocation we need to start finding the right types to relocate. We don't just want a load of dossers pumped full of happy pills pulling up their floorboards looking for treasure. We need quality. That's where the professor can help us out. But I figured we could run down to the court and see some of them in the flesh, see them for ourselves, judge who we think is piazza material.' He dropped the stirrer into the bin provided and looked up in a moment of cogitation. 'OK, less like research.' he said after consideration. 'More like we're auditioning them.'

14

The sleek black motor was already on the concrete jetty as it came into sight from the barge, rounding the last canal bend.

'Bollocks.' said Spence. 'We late?'

Roger shrugged, smiled. 'Five minutes, maybe.'

Roger didn't think it mattered. *What's it matter?* he asked himself, enjoying the cool breeze on his face stirred up by the boat's gentle progress. The latest batch of dope Darren had sold him was far and away the best he'd smoked. Combined with the couple of vodka sharpeners he'd had late afternoon and the amphetamine he'd been experimenting with to counter his lack of sleep, it left him feeling alert and relaxed. A good cocktail. He thought at that moment that it was possible to buy happiness. Next to him, Spence was a bundle of nerve endings, perched on the stern of the boat, ready to jump off at the first opportunity. When he did, he landed awkwardly, almost twisting his ankle. By the time Roger had languidly extracted himself, Spence was already at the car door, opening it up.

'Can I help you out?' he asked the woman inside, offering her a hand as she swooped out. Roger slowly scanned her. Late twenties, long legs in boots and a short skirt, long straight blonde hair. Big eyes, full lips. Tasty and knew it. He shoved both hands into his pockets.

On the far side of the car the head of a man, thick black hair with a side parting, appeared. Spence dropped the girl's hand and went around to greet him.

'Mr Penfold.' he said, shaking him by the hand. 'Pleasure to see you. I'm Spence. We met once, over the licensing matter. If you remember.'

'Vaguely.' said Penfold defensively. Reference to the licensing matter clearly wasn't that welcome.

'If I can introduce you to my colleague, Roger Merrion.' he said, ushering him around the car. Roger was faced with a short man, in a black polo-neck sweater and a tight-fitting leather jacket, pleated serge trousers and slip-ons. 'Roger, this is Maurice Penfold, business manager for Civic Radio. And this?' he queried, looking across at the girl, who was staring at the barge, her features twisted into a scowl.

'My partner, Lee.'

'We're not out here for a fucking river-boat shuffle, are we?' she squealed.

'No.' assured Spence. 'Just a means of transport to get us to our destination. There are drinks on board.'

'We're in the fucking middle of nowhere here.' she insisted, a nasty thought dawning on her. 'What if they're going to kidnap us?'

Penfold, as a senior executive of the region's top commercial radio station, looked as if he gave this serious credence.

'I'm always interested in new experiences, Mr—'

'Spence. Spence is fine.'

'I've always been at the cutting edge of events in this city. But this secrecy is all—'

'I hear what you're saying, but trust me. Everything will become clear, if you just bear with us. You're going to witness something genuinely original and exciting. We're really delighted that you've come along. It's important for us that what we're doing here is seen by the—' he held it for a second '—opinion formers.'

Over the top, thought Roger, who couldn't remember seeing Spence trying so hard. But Penfold was obviously a sucker for this kind of bollocks, letting his guard drop for Spence to hit him with the real message.

'I think the licensing matter proves I can be taken seriously.'

Lee clicked her tongue, swung her weight on to one hip. Provocatively, Roger thought. 'We could have gone to London this weekend.' she huffed, tossing her hair.

Spence pounced. 'Believe me, Miss. What you're going to see tonight, you can't find in London. They can't match this in London. No way.'

Lee clearly found that hard to believe but Penfold's bearing suggested no immediate departure. Instead, his mind perhaps still on the licensing matter, he moved to the back of the car and opened the boot, pulling out a folded metal contraption, four rubber wheels at one end.

'I hope you don't mind.' he said, 'but I brought someone from the station along with me. He insisted on coming.' added Penfold with a twitch of the mouth.

He carried the equipment to the front passenger seat, where he struggled with it for a moment before stepping back to open the door. 'You ready?' he asked whoever was inside.

Next to Roger, Lee shivered.

'Pervert.' she said. 'I hate him.'

Her proximity excited Roger, adding another layer to his general sense of wellbeing. Happiness bred confidence in him. He gave her a crooked smile and blinked slowly. He thought that she almost smiled back before he looked down at her legs.

'Like your boots.' he told her.

Now she gave him a proper glance, pouted her lips slightly. 'Thanks. Got them in London.'

Roger nodded in awe then blinked slowly. 'You like to smoke dope?' he asked her.

She looked at him a little more closely. 'Why? You got some?'

'Yeah. Got some.'

'Nice one. Just promise me you won't give any to this fucking creep.'

She looked back across towards the car from where Penfold emerged, pushing what turned out to be a folding wheelchair. Sitting in it was an older man, his well-used face suggesting more than sixty years, chopstick-thin in a red denim jacket, tight jeans and black cowboy boots. He wore a bandanna around his head, with his yellow hair pulled back into a painfully tight ponytail. A large pair of sunglasses completed the sense of a country-and-western star on hunger strike. But the identity of this listing, gurning figure wasn't a mystery. Roger had seen the same face, a little more *compos mentis* admittedly and with the headphones round his neck, staring at him from the back of many a bus during the rush hour.

'Everyone.' said Penfold. 'You may know Johnny Odom. He was at a loose end…' he added, tailing off with an air of apology.

'What's this?' croaked the invalid. 'Come to fucking drown me, have you, Maurice? Going to dispose of my body, never to be found again? Good enough for Jimmy Hoffa, good enough for me. Just make it quick, that's all I ask you. Just make it quick for old Johnny.'

Spence couldn't quite hide his displeasure at a gatecrasher, at *this* gatecrasher, but at his bidding Roger escorted the three of them into the barge. Getting Odom's wheelchair up the ramp had proved difficult, so Roger had carried him up over his shoulder, his body weight so small as to be almost negligible, like a bag of plastic footballs. Sitting in the cabin, as they were served drinks from the well-stocked bar, Roger hurriedly rolled a spliff and, despite Lee's earlier protestations, offered it around. Penfold calmly refused but Odom was happy to suck on it as if it were a straw in a can of pop before remembering to hand it on to Lee. Rather than being mellowed by the narcotic, he went into overdrive, sparing the others the strain of conversation by embarking on a monologue about the great waterways of their industrial past until Lee gigglingly pointed out that she didn't have an industrial past.

'Oh you're wrong there, love.' he moaned, rolling on the bench Roger had rested him on like Ray Charles at the piano, the healthy slug of Jack Daniel's in his plastic cup never quite spilling out. 'Everyone in this town has an industrial past. We all have that in common. We are an industrial people. Captains of industry or the poor bastards who slogged for them every day. Like my father and his father before him. The grist of the industrial machine, crushed in the cogs and gears of greed and oppression. This town was built on the bones of the workers and don't you forget it.'

Odom's voice filled the cabin, somehow fitting the environment of deeply grained wood that Norman had worked wonders to restore. Roger recognised the dogma that his father liked to spout, but he had had none of Odom's rhetorical gift. And the voice itself. Roger couldn't help but be impressed by it, sensed that it took all of Odom's energy to maintain its fruity tone, that his body had had to be sacrificed, a mere vessel for the porterage of its dark timbre.

'You speak for yourself.' said Lee, taking another dainty tug on the spliff. 'I'm more, you know, London.'

'Like hell you are. You can take the girl out of Gildenhall Side, but you can't take Gildenhall Side out of the girl.' He jabbed a finger at her. 'Doesn't matter how much Prada you wear, love, you've still got the mouth of a boilermaker's daughter.'

Penfold uncrossed his legs. 'Johnny. Enough.'

Odom screwed up his face. 'Maurice. That's a compliment. From me, Maurice, that's an absolute compliment. I helped rebuild this city. I'm part of its history. Proud of it.' He reverted to Lee. 'Don't be ashamed of what you are, darling. Only be ashamed of denying it.'

She cocked her head to one side. 'I'm not ashamed of who I am, am I, Maury?'

'You have nothing to be ashamed of.' Penfold assured her.

'Of course not. Let's not fall out, love.' said Odom, patting his knee. 'Why don't you come over here and give Uncle Johnny a cuddle?'

In his state of calm detachment, Roger was interested to see what happened next but they were interrupted by a second wave of guests. As another four stooped into the cabin, rendering it poky now rather than intimate, a number of acquaintances were renewed among the local glitterati. Roger suddenly felt he was at the centre of things, that he had a window, albeit slightly hazy (the stuff Darren had sold him *was* seriously strong, he had to admit), on the lifestyles of the rich and famous. It dawned on him how much Marion would have appreciated this, how hard she would have tried to fit in.

At the top of the stairs leading downwards, he saw Spence motioning him to come up on deck. Grinning stupidly at Lee, who winked at him, he began to clamber unsurely up, where darkness had fallen.

'Everything all right down there?' Spence asked.

'Fine. As far as I could tell.'

Spence gave Odom's wheelchair a gentle kick.

'Not happy about him fetching up. He's trouble.'

'You think?'

'I fucking know…he's connected. Friend of the McNallys.'

Roger stuck out his bottom lip. The McNallys were supposed to be nasty bastards, ran drugs through the city. Roger had never met one of them.

'That's why he can spout that shit on the radio, even though they've wanted to axe him for years.' Spence explained. 'That's why he can show up anywhere he likes and nobody tells him to fuck off. They're all afraid of him.'

'Him?'

'How do you think he got through prison? They took care of him and now he looks out for them where he still has influence.'

'Who's he got influence with?'

'You'd be surprised. He took the fall for lots of people. Johnny Odom's little black book could inconvenience lots of people if he ever decided to open it.' He breathed out hard through his nose. 'Not happy about it. Let's hope he gets so pissed he can't remember how to get here.'

They disembarked and headed for Goossens along the already well-defined path. The only potential difficulty was threatened by Odom's wheelchair on the iffy terrain but, keen to keep up, he found the will to use his own legs, undaunted even by the stairs up to the third floor. Roger hung back and brought up the rear, marvelling at the sagging backside on the broadcaster's jeans. Approaching the entrance, he noticed that the girl, Lee, was still waiting to follow the rest, apparently looking for something in her handbag. As he met her, she looked up, mouth sculpted into a laconic smile.

'Sorry, I've forgotten your name.' she said.

'Roger.'

'Roger.' she repeated, cocking her head to one side. 'Roger by name…'

'Lee.' he said.

'That's me.' she giggled. 'Like it?'

He made a point of looking her up and down.

'Like it all.' he told her, taking a step towards her. She placed the flat of her hand on his sternum but didn't push him back.

'Nice eyes.' she said and looked at the gaping door. 'Why don't you show me the way…Roger?'

She turned inside and he followed, feeling no resistance as he let his hand rest firmly on the pleasing swell of her arse.

15

A WEEK LATER

Roger turned his mobile on as he left the ASBO hearing in courtroom number 2 and it buzzed almost immediately, telling him he had messages. He called his voicemail and listened in. There were three, all from Lee. The first was a cheery request for him to call, the second a more plaintive one along the same lines, but spoken in the baby voice that she resorted to regularly to get what she wanted. The third contained the first stirring of anger from a woman scorned. Roger didn't bother calling her. She'd ring again. Roger put her interest down to the burgeoning success of the Show and her need to bask in reflected glory, but he was as surprised by her persistent pursual of him as he was by his own take-it-or-leave-it attitude to her advances. The moments of being with her during the initial consummation of their affair had been pleasant enough. He had long ago given up on his dreams of getting into the knickers of girls like Lee, so had thrilled at the reality of being wanted by her, but away from her actual presence he had no longing for her. She was doing all the running and the less interest he showed the harder she came at him. Roger felt as if he had unwrapped the greatest mystery there was. Perhaps it was a little late for him now, but he had resolved to share the secret with Nick, the next time he spoke to him. Whenever that might be.

As he sought out Darren's number in his mobile's directory, the rest of the public gallery spilled out from court number 2. A group of about ten young men and women, shifting from foot to foot, leaning on each other or engaged in minor shoving games, hovered close to the door until one other, dressed like the rest of them in a tracksuit, his baseball cap just replaced on his head, emerged. They crowded around him, some offering him friendly punches. One tall, acne-ridden youth stood face to face with him and with a low growl of encouragement grabbed both his cheeks and pulled them hard. One wag knocked his cap off again, giving the girls in the group the chance to tousle his hair.

With his phone pressed to his ear, Roger looked on, marvelling at the speed of the chavs' evolutionary response to the purported sanction of the ASBO. They understood, at an instinctual level, how to spike the guns of authority. Here he was, looking on as the latest recipient was being *congratulated* by his contemporaries, most of whom (Roger knew for a fact) were already ordered up themselves. The ASBO had become a badge of honour among the pack society. It was simply *de rigueur*. Not to have one rendered you a nobody.

You had to like their style.

The person he was calling picked up.

'Darren.' said Roger into his phone. ''S me. Yeah…got another one for you.' He consulted the edge of his newspaper, where he had scribbled the details. 'Kelvin Maguire, 23 Mantua Road. Just been served by the magistrate. Five-year order…'

'What's his form ?' Darren asked.

'The usual. Likes setting fire to things. Nicking stuff. Foster parents want rid, so he'd be coming your way anyhow.'

He heard Darren yawn and stretch on the other end. 'All right. I think we've got a flatshare in Delius Grove that'll do him. He'll be an asset to the residents' committee. I'll recommend him for treasurer. With that I think we're pretty full up. Might as well knock it on the head for the day.'

'Fine. See you tonight?' Roger asked.

'Sure.'

'Could you…get me some more gear?'

'Yeah.' Darren groaned, reaching for something. 'What you after? Dope or speed this time?'

Roger ran a finger under his nose. 'Both.'

Darren hissed out a breath. 'You're getting through it, aren't you, mate?'

'Just a bit stressed right now. Need to keep myself going.'

'If you want, I can throw in something else for you. Freebie. Maybe it'll do the trick.'

'Yeah, sure. Cheers.'

Roger called off and shoved the mobile into the pocket of his coat. He was set to leave when a presence blocked his way.

'Well, well, well, if it isn't Roger the Dodger.'

Roger was faced by a big man, big in both height and girth. He wore black jeans and a blue leather jacket over a white nylon shirt, pretty much what he had worn when he worked for the council. His unwashed black hair had been flattened down, leaving an unintentional cowlick across his forehead. The beard and moustache were new and not yet fully formed, but the smell of fried food clinging to him hadn't changed.

'Dave Spalding.' said Roger, with no sense of celebration. 'What you up for today?'

Spalding snorted derisively. 'Upstanding citizen like me? Ooh no. I'm not one for brushing with the law. When I seen you, I thought you was the one in trouble. Not paying your council tax, is it?'

Roger didn't like the question, wouldn't have liked a rendition of 'Happy Birthday' if it came out of Spalding's slack mouth. 'I'm working.' said Roger. 'What about you?'

Spalding bent his knees slightly, jutted his chin out. 'I'm here for a friend. Lend a bit of moral support.'

'In trouble, is he, this friend of yours?'

'What can I tell you? A misunderstanding is all.'

Roger faked surprise. 'Another misunderstanding? Misunderstandings just seem to follow you around, Dave.'

Spalding stared but Roger sensed him consciously restraining himself.

'Well, when people are prepared to tell lies about you, things can be tricky.'

'So they were all telling lies? Bit of a coincidence, wouldn't you say? Bad luck to get sacked over a coincidence.'

'Not sacked. I resigned, remember?'

The stare of Spalding's cold blue eyes made Roger shiver. Spalding may have jumped before he was pushed, but the weight of evidence against him had been threatening to buckle the table legs of the Investigations Team. Spalding, it gradually emerged, had spent the last twenty years abusing his position on the Property Maintenance Team. The team was supposed to repair problems on council properties for free but, on any occasion he found the flat or house inhabited by a woman on her own, he had insisted on payment in kind. Typically allergic to any kind of scandal, the council had managed to keep a lid on it after Spalding had bailed out, effectively getting away scot-free.

'Still don't know who stitched me up,' Spalding commented, looking quickly over his shoulder. 'Still don't know who grassed me up.'

'Er, how about the thirty residents who said you raped them?'

But Spalding shook his head. 'How could anyone trust

those bitches? They're happy to believe stories about me and then slap one of your ASBOs on them the next day. You know what they're like, Roger. You wouldn't condemn a man from what they said.' He sniffed to signify the matter was closed, then bent down slightly to scratch the inside of his giant thigh. 'Work, you say?' he asked casually.

'ASBO stuff.' said Roger.

Spalding nodded in approval. 'Like it. Come down hard on these fucking scrotes. Make them jump.'

'I'm sure the team will be thrilled to have your endorsement.'

Spalding offered a joyless smile and watched Roger head out of the courthouse. 'See you soon.' he called, as if he meant it.

16

THREE WEEKS LATER

The mood on the third floor was one of quiet industry, occasionally interrupted by sudden moments of ear-splitting shrillness, emanating from the two large speakers that had been set up at either end of the window.

'Sorry.' said Mason, sitting cross-legged on the floor, quickly unplugging the wires that led into the small mixing desk positioned next to the canteen.

'Can't you shut that fucking thing up?' asked Maxine, the bomber jacket Spence had given her zipped up tight, not even bothering to look up from her copy of *Hot Goss*. 'They'll fucking hear that.'

'There aren't any instructions.' explained Mason. 'I've never done this before.' He looked up towards Roger, who stood, eyes wide, staring across the piazza. His attention drawn. In one of the vehicle parking bays underneath Bax Villas there was, exceptionally, a vehicle. A medium-sized red Ford Transit van, it looked in unnaturally good condition for its location. Roger's initial response was to think it had been nicked or maybe even put there deliberately by Spence to guarantee something for the first batch of customers, who would arrive in what could be a quiet time. But he soon realised that something else was afoot. Driving seat occupied and engine running, the van was being guarded by at least two men at all times, nervously keeping an eye out, while a number of others, possibly as many as half a dozen, came and went carrying boxes or large items of furniture. Roger knew it wasn't a burglary. Burglary could be performed at a much more leisurely pace than the frantic toing and froing he was witnessing. He looked on as the last boxes were loaded up and the majority of the group congregated around the back of the vehicle, waiting impatiently until the last of their number emerged, carrying an old lady in his arms. Roger recognised the dear in a chair he'd seen threatened on his first night. As she was put in the front seat, the others all piled into the back, slamming the doors shut as the van sped out and off the estate.

She'd made her escape – an unofficial relocation. He hadn't seen it happen before, but anecdotally he knew it wasn't the first. People were taking matters into their own hands. He'd tell the boys in Housing. Spence would be pleased – another empty flat to house with ASBO talent. Roger experienced a strange mix of emotion at observing this. He was glad to see that she had managed to get off, perhaps a little guilty that he'd done nothing to help her, as he had silently promised to do. Yet that wasn't quite it either.

He thought it might even be *nostalgia*. But, in truth, it was difficult to be certain. The amphetamine tablets Darren from Housing had suggested to combat Roger's gruelling two-job routine made everything seem as if it were happening to another person. The cocaine he'd recently starting experimenting with was better but a little harder to find.

'Rodge?' Mason was still asking for his attention.

'What?'

He waved the cables. 'You got any idea how you put this thing together?'

Roger didn't. As usual, Spence had had the stuff brought in and then just dumped for the rest of them to sort out. This time it was a public-address system he had got from the licensing enforcement section, which had impounded it from a crack house over Charlock way somewhere. Tonight was Mason's first night as official Show commentator, bringing his incomparable gift for chav punditry to the cocktail. Right now, though, he was having big problems with feedback.

'Do you have to make so much noise?'

Roger turned to see Lee standing at the door, arms wrapped around herself, shoulders hunched, wearing a T-shirt and a pair of boxer shorts that he recognised as belonging to him. Self-consciously ignoring the looks from Mason and the Housing guys on the sofa, she padded towards him at the window, brushing her long, slim legs against him.

'Hey.' she said, a little plaintively, cocking her head so her hair, which she considered to be her chief weapon, fell across her face and down over her shoulder. Rubbing her body briefly against his, she gave a little purr of pleasure.

'Been up long?' she asked.

'About five hours.'

'What's the time?'

He told her. Surprise flashed across her face for a moment but then disappeared.

'So.' she wanted to know, 'what we doing?'

Roger ignored her, choosing to drain the can of Red Blast in his hand, his third of the day. Lee had confirmed herself as the type who liked to attach themselves, and Roger still had moments, though only moments now, when he wondered why she had chosen him. But she claimed a genuine attraction. There was something about him, she had said. 'I like the quiet type.' she'd told him, throwing her hair around. 'You give off this aura of, like…dunno, experience, I suppose. Like you've seen a lot. You've seen a lot, haven't you, babes?'

Despite these reassurances, watching her naked, rolling a post-coital joint as she sat straddled over him, he was overwhelmed with the sense of being an impostor in the realisation of his own fantasy. But Lee, with her variety of black lingerie, her gymnastic body, her foul mouth, belonged to the world of fantasy, and Roger had quickly become comfortable there with her. It was outside that world, like out on the third floor in the presence of others, that he disliked her, thought everything she said was laughable. But her mere vicinity was enough to stir an angry arousal in him. They fucked often, Roger quick to realise that tender lovemaking was something she disdained. He would have preferred to have her locked up in his room upstairs, ready for him whenever he wanted it. Something told him she wouldn't demur. A type of victimhood was her appeal.

There had been little comment from any of the others about it, as if such an easy and apparently triumphant conquest was perfectly natural for Roger. This was testament to how much he had changed. Or they had changed. Or they had all changed. The arrangement was just accepted. In fact, the derogatory remarks one or two of the others had made about her, referring to her as his 'Labrador', had only gone to confirm a sense of normality about the attachment. Roger had been concerned about Penfold's response to her defection, but on the two or three times he had returned to the Show he had been civil, introducing him to her successor, a brunette with a tight smile who reminded Roger of Lorraine, the CostBlast vamp of his dreams.

Roger didn't answer Lee's question but told her to get dressed.

'What do you want me to put on?' she asked, so that everyone could hear.

'Black dress. One of the girls has gone sick. You can do some waitressing tonight.'

The slight was intended. She pushed out a hip and turned her mouth, but he met her eye and stared her down. 'Wanker.' she told him before sweeping out. Roger turned back to the piazza with a long blink. She liked the drama, but they both knew she'd do his bidding.

Mason had tentatively plugged two more cables together and the result was not another screech but a promising hum from the speakers. He picked up a microphone nearby and switched it on, two taps with his fingers on its head picked up and amplified.

'Excellent, in business.' he commented.

'About fucking time.' murmured Maxine.

'One, two.' Mason spoke into the microphone. 'Testing, one, t…Who are you?'

An unfamiliar, furtive presence at the doorway drew attention. For a moment everyone froze, even Lee, who hadn't quite made it to the door and stood only a few paces away.

The girl in the doorway wore a pair of track pants and a light grey waterproof cagoule. A mane of curly red hair had been inexpertly bundled upwards, away from a pale face with a tendency towards puffiness. The girl's eyes, strikingly green even at a moment's glance, danced quickly around the room. With a sudden motion she placed both hands against the lintel and pushed herself off in an attempt to get away.

She might have been quick but Maxine was off her chair quicker, flying out on to the landing just as the girl reached the top of the stairs. Maxine was Security, so there was professional pride at stake. Even so, thought Roger as he moved towards the door, he thought it was risky to rugby-tackle the girl and send them both flying down the steps together. By the time he and the others had crowded around their launch pad, Maxine had taken control of the situation and stood over the girl, one foot planted hard on her windpipe. Roger could see the blood welling up in one of the girl's nostrils.

'Who the fuck are you?' Maxine wanted to know, offering a slight release of pressure.

The girl moaned. 'I've broken my leg.'

Maxine stepped down again. 'I asked you a question.'

'I've broken me fucking leg, you fucking bitch!'

Maxine calmly stooped down and put a hand to the girl's calf, planting the other one on her mouth as she uttered a shriek of authentic agony.

'Who are you?' insisted Maxine, preparing to ratchet up the pain to find out.

'Enough.' said Roger, emerging from the group above them and walking down the stairs. He motioned for Maxine to step back but she initially stood firm.

'We have to find out who she is.' she growled.

'OK, but let's not stoop to torture, shall we?'

Maxine looked down the next flight, exasperated. 'There could be others…'

'I understand the seriousness of it.' snapped Roger. 'I just don't want—'

'There's nobody else.' said the girl, her face contorted. 'I'm on my own.'

Roger looked at Maxine for some acknowledgement that he had been right. She gave him none.

'How the fuck did she get in here?' This was Lee, shouting from above.

'How'm I supposed to know?' asked Maxine.

'You're supposed to be Security, aren't you?'

'Fuck off.' screamed Maxine, threatening to start up the stairs until Roger grabbed her by the elbow.

'I want you to go down and check the entrance, make sure there's nobody else. OK?' She was still but Roger felt the resistance in her sinews. 'OK?' he repeated with greater intensity.

Maxine made to go downstairs, stopped on the first step, gestured up towards Lee. 'I don't care who your fucking tart is. I can make her ugly in a fucking hurry.'

Roger didn't doubt it. As Maxine descended, he lowered himself down to the girl's level.

'How old are you?' he asked. A strange first question, he realised, but looking at her he found himself thinking about Beth.

She swallowed. 'Fifteen.'

'Your leg…?'

'It really hurts.'

'OK. We'll get you some help. What's your name?'

'Maddy.'

'How did you get in, Maddy?'

'I went in the shaft…' She winced. 'My leg. I'll fucking kill that bitch…'

'The shaft.' Roger said. 'Then what?'

'I climbed through a vent thing and came through at the top.'

'Nobody else saw you?'

'Fucking hell! Nobody saw me. I've broken me fucking leg here. And I'm supposed…' She remembered something and her demeanour suddenly changed. 'I'm having a baby. I'm having a baby. If I've lost my baby…'

She tried to get up but the first hint of weight on her leg made her collapse. Roger hauled her up by the armpits.

'Can I get some help down here?' he asked of the statues at the top of the stairs. Mason and one of the Housing boys traipsed down. 'Get her up to my room.' Roger instructed them as they hauled her up.

'Where am I supposed to go?' asked Lee. But Roger brushed by her and headed to the canteen, where his mobile phone lay on the counter. He called Spence.

17

That night, Spence and Roger stood at the counter amid the chatter, drinking coffee but not saying much. The last boat of revellers for the night were coming in to make up what was another full house. Spence waved and smiled at a few of the regulars, even acknowledging the ubiquitous presence of Johnny Odom, hunched across one side of his chair, talking to Lee as she in turn glanced across at Roger.

'She wants me to have him barred.' Roger said matter-of-factly.

'Believe me, I fucking wish. You think we've got trouble now with this fucking girl, wait until we tried that. He keeps talking about bringing his mates over—' He lifted his hands and signified inverted commas with his fingers '—to discuss business arrangements.'

'Meaning?'

'What do you think? Meaning the fucking McNallys.'

They were interrupted as Mason's voice emerged from the twin speakers in a singsong tone, with a detectable increase in numbers approaching the window as he spoke.

'OK, just coming out on to the piazza in the distinguishing red trainers, passing the swings…now…we have Gary Naylor. Gary should be well known to you if you've been to the Show before. Gary lives in Delius Grove and he was one of our first in the city to receive an Antisocial Behaviour Order a couple of years back following an aggravated attack on a mobile library that took a wrong turn. Since then, Gazbo, as he's known to his friends, has breached his order on – let me check – five separate occasions for offences including glue-sniffing and public indecency. He currently has a backlog of a thousand pounds in fines payable to the magistrates' court, which he pays off at two quid a week. Gary is a registered methadone addict and is currently engaged in a relationship with Shania Redpath, also of Delius Grove, which Social Services have characterised as being "mutually abusive." Hopefully, Shania should be out a bit later on and we can see them in action together. Should be worth waiting for…'

Mason put down the mike and returned to a couple of young men, whose specific questions he was happy to answer.

Roger tapped Spence on the arm as a middle-aged man approached them, having just entered the room.

'Gentlemen.' he said, running a hand down the back of his head.

'Doctor.' said Spence. 'What's the verdict?'

'Definitely a break. Clean one, probably. I've done what I can with what's available here. It should heal but that'll take time. I ought,' he said, breathing out hard, 'to recommend that she be moved but…'

'Yeah, we'd better think about that.'

'I mean, if she went to hospital, there'd be questions…Wouldn't want to jeopardise things here, not when people enjoy it so much…'

'Exactly.' said Spence with a sober nod. 'Exactly.'

'Perhaps I could make arrangements with some people at the health authority. They're…you know, trustworthy. I could arrange for some more medical equipment to be brought over.'

'And the baby?'

The doctor shrugged. 'Difficult to say. If she is pregnant, it's the early stages. There are no outward signs of any trauma connected with the fall…'

They were silent for a moment.

'Well.' said the doctor, 'if that's all I can help you with.'

'No, thanks a million.' said Roger, planting a hand on his shoulder and beckoning Lee over. 'Could you make sure Dr and Mrs Gilbert are looked after? Free drinks tonight.'

The doctor didn't notice Lee's dirty look but she led the physician away as requested.

'Blimey. Got her eating out of your hand.' commented Spence.

Roger was unresponsive but, as often happened, he felt giddy at the power he seemed to have over her, the sense that reminded him why he had anything to do with her.

'So what? We keep Maddy here?' he asked.

'Who?'

'Maddy. The girl.'

Spence looked at him with a hint of disapproval. 'She's local, is she?'

Roger nodded. 'Arne Villas.'

'Parents?'

'Lives with her mother.'

'Where's the daddy?'

'Identity unknown. Stepfather doing time for GBH.'

Spence thought about it for a moment. 'If she goes back, how do we know she's going to keep her mouth shut.'

'She won't.'

'How do you know that?'

'It's what she told me.'

'She said she'd cough us up?'

'She doesn't want to go back, Spence. She's up the duff…'

Spence groaned, squeezed his forehead.

'…her mother's a total pillhead. She's trying to get away. That's why she was here – she was looking for a place to squat.'

Spence was incredulous. 'She wants to run away but she doesn't think of getting off the estate? You believe that?'

Roger wasn't sure. 'I don't know. Limited horizons. She said she'd blow us wide open if we kick her out.'

'What about school?'

'Fucking hell. Be serious.'

Spence sighed. 'Three weeks to mend…' He sucked on his bottom lip. 'And, what, we hope Mum's too off her face to notice?'

'Then we find her somewhere to go. On the quiet.'

'And then she'll keep shtum.'

'That's what she's said.'

Spence nodded outside, where Gary Naylor was living up to Mason's billing, throwing a paving stone through the back windscreen of a hearse they had planted on the piazza in a typical taboo-testing stunt. 'She's one of them, man.'

Roger disagreed. 'I don't think so. She wants out of it. She wants out of the life down there.'

'You seem to know a lot about her.'

'We just talked. She's a nice kid.'

Spence appeared doubtful but resigned. 'Doesn't sound like we have much of a choice. But you're taking responsibility for her.'

'Sure.' agreed Roger, putting his mug down on the counter and sliding it to the girl behind the counter whose name he had forgotten. 'She can go into one of the other flats that we're painting up.'

'They're supposed to be for the use of paying guests.'

'One less shag parlour won't make any difference.'

Spence had been quick to cotton on to the erotic response

that the Show had on certain couples and had decided to cash in by offering suitable short-term accommodation.

'This is business, Rodge.' he had to remind him. 'Letting her stay is a business decision. That's all.'

'Course.'

'We start giving them pet names down there, we might as well pack up.'

He wanted to drive the point home but was distracted by Maxine waving across at them from the door. Spence peered to get a better look at the large man standing next to her.

'What's that cunt doing here?' he wanted to know and headed off to find out. Roger turned to see the unwelcome figure of Dave Spalding. On top of his grubby history, Spence had a personal animus for Spalding and he looked on, expecting the fat man to get his marching orders. But he saw Spalding take the initiative, explaining something to Spence, who, though not happy, responded by ushering him on to the third floor and towards Roger.

'Hey, Roger, you remember Dave Spalding. What were you in, Dave, vermin control, wasn't it?'

'Property maintenance.' corrected Spalding.

'Sorry.' said Spence. 'Dave's found a new line of work since his career with the council.'

'We meet again.' Spalding addressed Roger with a grin. 'People will start to talk.' He looked around. 'So, this got anything to do with your…work?'

'What do you want?' Roger asked, aware of a curious reticence on Spence's part to join him.

'Came to have a look around. Now I see what you were doing at the court. You've been busy. Might want to take it easy for a while.' he added, cocking his head. 'You look like shit.'

Lee chose her moment well to glide past. Without warning,

Roger grabbed her around the waist, pulled him to her and kissed her violently on the mouth. She, as he knew she would, reciprocated, pushing her loins against his, searching for his tongue with her own, their mouths locked together, pumping away like a pulsing heart for a few moments before he broke it off and flung her aside.

'Not bad for a bloke who looks like shit.' Roger said to Spalding. 'Bit better than having to shag old ladies halfway to hypothermia who'll do just about anything to get their central heating back on.'

Spalding stepped at him with intent. 'You'd better watch that fucking mouth of yours. It's going to land you in serious trouble.'

Roger just gave Spalding a heavy-eyed smile. It was Spence who stepped in between them. 'Leave it.' he exhorted Spalding. 'No trouble.'

'I'll be waiting.' said Spalding, allowing himself to be drawn away but stabbing a finger at Roger. 'You'll make a mistake and I'll be waiting.'

Spence took Spalding towards the bar, looking back to gave Roger a meaningful stare.

'Come and have a drink.' he asked him. But Roger shook his head and walked out.

Maddy was watching TV in Roger's room when he went in to see her. She didn't switch it off. Roger sat down on a chair next to the bed, uncomfortably conscious of the evidence of Lee's presence there.

There was a natural history programme on when he sat down but Maddy was clicking through the cable channels at the rate of about one every three seconds.

'How are you feeling?' he asked her.

'What?' she asked over the sound of a music video she found worth a longer look.

'How's your leg?'

'What do you think? It fucking hurts.' she said, clicking her tongue.

Roger nodded. 'Of course.'

He waited for her to speak.

'This where you live?' she asked.

'At the moment.'

'They're knocking this place down.'

'Maybe not.'

She pointed the remote lazily and blanked the screen.

'So can I stay here?'

'Yes, until your leg heals. Then I'll get you out, off the estate.'

She made no response.

'That's what you wanted?' Roger checked.

'I want to have my baby and I don't want that cow anywhere near it.'

'Your mother? She's the reason you're…'

'I fucking hate her.'

'Doesn't she treat you very well?'

'I fucking hate her, all right?' she snapped. 'She won't even care I'm gone.'

With the TV off, the sounds from the third floor drifted up.

'So what do you lot do here?'

Roger shrugged. 'We watch.'

'Watch what?'

'People.'

'What people?'

'The people out there. On the estate.'

She sneered. 'What's the fucking point of that?'

The question stung Roger. He wasn't sure he could answer, other than to say it was making him rich. 'It's difficult to explain.' he managed. 'People behave differently here. It's interesting.'

'Sounds boring to me.'

'What do you like to do?' he asked.

She eyed him unsurely. 'What you mean?'

'I mean…I don't know…you like reading?'

'I can read.'

'What do you like to read?'

She had a quick answer ready but checked herself, took a moment to measure a response. 'I don't know. Whatever.'

'Do you want me to get you some books?'

'Yeah.' she said, looking down. 'That would…yeah, cheers.'

'Which ones? Anything in particular?'

She shifted her weight in the bed. 'You choose.'

'OK. I will.'

She looked across at the unpacked boxes that still contained the volumes of Marx. 'Those ones any good?'

Roger smiled. 'No. You wouldn't like them.'

She gave him a tight smile back.

'You should rest.'

'Yeah.' she agreed, switching the telly back on.

'You want something to eat or something?'

'I'm a bit thirsty. Wouldn't mind a drink.'

'Sure.' said Roger, standing up. 'What would you like?'

She looked up hopefully. 'Bacardi Breezer?'

Roger went down to the bar to get Maddy the can of Coke she had reluctantly accepted as a compromise. He had used her pregnancy as a reason to refuse her any alcohol, but he knew there was more to it than that. He had to do what he could to keep her straight. He asked for the can and a treble vodka for himself, splash of tonic, no more.

She wanted to get away. In her was the will to escape the Composers'. To Roger, for whom so much that was once obvious had become confused, this seemed a beacon of clarity, a priceless commodity. Somewhere inside him, Roger felt a dull urge to get away: the urge he'd had all his life was starting to return. It didn't matter where you were going, it was the act of escape that counted.

Roger leaned with his back to the bar and took a large swig of vodka, swilled it around his mouth and gulped it down. Lee swept past on her high heels, pointedly ignoring him. Roger was repelled by the urgency of his own carnal desire for her and the private knowledge that what he really wanted was for her to try and resist him.

Across the room, he was annoyed to see Spalding still there, still talking to Spence, giving him inexplicable attention. Odom stopped next to them for a brief word, then set himself off with a push on his wheels. His momentum brought him to the bar, alongside Roger. He ordered a drink, instructing the barmaid to put it on his tab.

'Roger.' he said, spinning his chair to face out to the room.

'Johnny.' replied Roger, suggesting in his delivery that he didn't want to engage in conversation.

'Full house again.' Odom commented. 'Business goes well. In rude health.'

'Spence has a gift for organisation.'

Johnny considered the comment for a moment. 'You're not wrong, son. You're not wrong. A gift. A gift is exactly what it is…Spence is a man of practical talents. But you know what I see when I see the two of you. You know what's obvious to see with the two of you?'

Roger sighed. 'What?'

'You're the one with the vision. You're the one looking for something out there—' he gestured to the window '—that nobody else can see. Nobody, that is.' he said, pausing to take a slurp through a straw, 'except me.'

Roger looked across at him.

'I was the same as you. At least, what I think you were

like…before. I wore a suit for thirty years, paid my dues, toed the line. Where did it get me? Five of your earth years at Her Majesty's Pissoir, that's where. But it was prison that made me see the light about things, set me off on the path towards…experience. You have to have something that triggers it off, open up your eyes to what really matters.'

Roger found himself speaking, almost involuntarily. 'My father.' he said. 'He died. I don't think he ever enjoyed himself for one moment the whole time I knew him. He never took a risk. I didn't want to…'

He stopped but Johnny was nodding sympathetically.

'I saw it in your eyes the first time I met you. You're starting late, like I did. But you know what? That makes you better equipped for the journey.' Johnny pivoted himself, looked straight up at Roger. 'It's an odyssey. A journey of discovery, only for the brave few. You'll carry people in your wake. That's why.' he commented, as Lee passed by them both at a distance carrying a silver tray, 'you get trim like that throwing themselves at your feet. Back yourself to go all the way. Free yourself. Trust me, it's worth it.'

Roger was transfixed by Odom's cobra stare for a minute. In his eyes, like his voice, there was still a vestige of the fire that had consumed the rest of him up. Then it was gone as Johnny's face gurned itself into an ugly smile.

'So.' he said. 'That girl. You going to send her back down, feed her to the lions?'

'Haven't decided.'

'Interested to hear what you do with her. Keep me informed, won't you?' He set off again, rolling back towards Spence and Spalding, who appeared to be bringing their conversation to a close. 'How old did she say she was?' he called back, but Roger didn't reply. He finished his own drink and took the Coke through to Maddy. They watched CostBlast together for a while until he could stand watching Lorraine no longer and, with Odom's comments throbbing like a headache around him, went to curtail Lee's working night in favour of his own pressing needs.

18

EIGHT DAYS LATER

Roger saw the arrival of the lone police car as it followed the road around the piazza. For another vehicle its meandering pace could have suggested threat or fear. Visits from the police were becoming something of a rarity now. With virtually every right-minded citizen off the estate either with Housing's help or on their own initiative, there wasn't anybody left who would think of calling the Old Bill, except for a laugh or because they wanted a family member taken away.

It was still morning. Roger was fooling himself into thinking that he might show up at work, then into thinking he might call in sick. But calling in would only draw attention to his lengthy absence. Spence had assured him that Maxine and Mason were covering for him. He wasn't really sure whether the council were still paying him, although there was no reason to suppose they weren't.

So he watched, nursing a can of lager that had been warming in his hand for a while now. Roger had come to enjoy watching the piazza in the mornings, once the contract refuse collectors in Spence's pay had done their daily clean-up from the night before. Ironic that the residents on the Composers' were the best served in terms of rubbish collection in the entire municipal region. They even had a Sunday pick-up.

There wasn't much happening usually but there was still the occasional incident to savour, the real spontaneous sort that Roger liked, however minor. A few truants watched the pig car go by, choosing to ignore it apart from the obligatory offensive gestures in its direction. A small rebellion, but somehow honest, Roger felt. So different from the contrivance of the evening sessions, changed now with Spence's constant attempts at artificial escalation.

'Got to keep them guessing. Got to keep surprising them.' Spence said a lot of the time. The latest innovation had been the introduction of the Doguns, a clan of asylum seekers who needed six flats to house their entire number. The Doguns had been relocated by the Home Office out of London and had a reputation for being 'eccentric'. Spence had whipped them in the moment he got wind of them, with excellent results. Wherever they had come from was obviously an excellent training ground for their new home. They had instinctively understood the terms of engagement on the Composers', treated it like a theme park, and had met aggression with equal aggression, their numbers allowing them the luxury of ruthless retribution. A series of tit-for-tat arson attacks had cost Spence a lot in overtime payments for the Renovations Team but he was more than happy to pay it.

Ultimately, the new outlanders had earned a grudging respect from the rest on the estate, especially after they had brought a goat out on to the piazza, then slaughtered and cooked it on a spit to celebrate some obscure festival. Now, as big wheels in the increasingly popular dogfighting scene on the piazza, their position appeared secure.

But the Doguns divided opinion on the third floor. There

were some who preferred to see the piazza ruled by the indigenous tribes like the Clamms or the Moriartys. 'They're absolute scum.' Roger had overheard one woman, part of a group of legal secretaries out on a birthday bash, say, 'but at least they're our scum.' Others, perhaps those of a more liberal bent, generally rooted for the Kurdish family, enjoying the fact that they gave as good as they got. Some regular wags had even taken to wearing T-shirts bearing a likeness to Calendar Dogun, the sociopath son of the family head. Like everything else, this had inspired Spence, who had hurriedly set up his own line in Show wear. A batch of T-shirts bearing a cross-eyed photo of star delinquent Wayne Morphy and the caption 'Gizzit' had sold out in a matter of days.

The police car parked up and two male officers emerged with a palpable air of professional seriousness. Roger watched them as they climbed the stairs at the exterior of Arne Villas and headed along the third level of entrances. Roger's jaw tightened as they stopped at a faded red door with two ply panels where windows had once been. As one of the coppers knocked, the other cast an edgy glance in both directions. Roger picked up the binoculars from one of the seats nearby and put them to his eyes.

The door opened a few inches and a conversation ensued, the policemen trying to negotiate their way in. Eventually, the door was pulled back just far enough to let them slip through. Roger caught a brief glance of a scrawny female figure, hair dyed an implausible crow black, as she shut the door after them. He lowered the binoculars.

There could be only one reason why Maddy's mother had called the police.

The preparations for that evening's Show were temporarily suspended as the crew crowded around the portable telly Roger had set up.

The local newsreader was a frequent visitor to the third floor and couldn't mention the Composers' without the wry lifting of an eyebrow.

Roger had seen the TV crew arrive and do a hasty interview with Mrs Marsh, which had started calmly enough but soon descended into a tirade of abuse, with her jabbing her finger at the cameraman, forcing him to step back along the balcony until he had almost fallen down the steps behind him. As he watched the TV now, Roger was getting that first-person view of Maddy's mother, the tears that had run down her face leaving trails in her make-up, her face contorted with fundamentalist rage. Spence turned the sound up.

'Whoever you are, you sick *bleep*ing pervert, whoever you are that's holding on to my baby, I just want you to know that I'm *bleep*ing coming to get you, you *bleep*ing *bleep*, and when I find you, I'm going to cut off your *bleep*ing *bleep* and shove it up your *bleep*ing *bleep*.' Then came a low sob and Mrs Marsh crumpled into the arms of a fat neighbour. 'My baby, my baby, just give me back my baby…'

The screen reverted to the newsreader, who was affirming Roger's opinion of him as a smug bastard. 'The deputy chief constable, Jim Maxwell, made this plea at a news conference held a short time later.'

Cut to a black-haired, grey-bearded man in uniform, reading woodenly from a prepared statement, eyes occasionally flashing up at the camera.

'We urge anyone who has any knowledge or information or has seen anything suspicious or otherwise or anything they think is relevant to this enquiry to contact us.'

An unflatteringly gormless photo of Maddy appeared on screen with a phone number beneath it. 'Police are on full alert for any sightings of Madelaine, last seen in a grey shell suit.' said the newsreader, before moving on to a story about CCTV cameras being installed in every GP's surgery in the city.

Norman, on a rare visit up to the third floor, made a face and looked for somewhere to stub out his rolly. 'No reward.' he commented. 'Tight bastards. You think she'd be worth fifty quid or something.'

Spence turned the box off and looked across at Roger with eyebrows raised interrogatively. 'Well?'

Roger huffed. 'Everyone looking for her…We'll have to keep her here for the minute.'

'Maybe we should have got her out before.'

'Her leg's nearly mended. There was no need to. I'd assumed…'

Spence shook his head sadly, lifted his arms to the heavens. 'I know, I know. Who the fuck waits ten days before telling the police her kid's gone missing?'

Roger didn't have an answer but one came from the doorway.

'She probably thought I was at my gran's.' said Maddy, standing in the doorway on the crutches Dr Gilbert had kindly provided in the job lot of medical equipment.

'And where does she live?' asked Spence snappily.

'On the estate.'

Spence just shrugged for effect. 'I love these people.' he commented before turning back to Maddy as she hobbled in on her sticks. 'So what do you want to do now?' he asked her. 'Everyone's looking out for you.'

'How do you mean?'

'Your mother's managed to get round to telling the police that you've disappeared. Your picture's just been on the telly.'

'Really?'

'I wouldn't get excited.' Norman told her, finally resorting to putting his fag butt in his shirt pocket. 'You looked strangely…bloated.'

Roger stepped towards her protectively. 'Your mother did

say she wanted you back. Sounded like she meant it.'

But Maddy shook her head. 'She's lying. She just wants the attention. I've told you. I'm not going back. You put me back out there and you know what I'll do.' She raised herself back on the crutches and moved away from Roger, towards Spence. 'I can help out.' she told him. 'I can help with the cleaning.'

The silence that followed wasn't promising. She swung back towards Roger, put one hand to her stomach.

'For the baby. I just want what's best for the baby. Don't send my baby down there.'

'Like mother, like daughter.' muttered Mason.

The parallel was one that hadn't escaped what remained of Roger's rational side.

'Now we've got the Old Bill crawling all over the place...'

Roger knew it wasn't a good situation. But he found the thought of abandoning her back out on the estate almost too much to bear, just one manifestation of a fattening streak of sentimentality growing inside him. Any memory of his own children threatened to make him burst into tears.

He knew it was difficult for the others to understand, but in his own moral abseil down the face of reason, protecting this fat, ugly girl seemed important beyond reason.

'She stays.' he said to them. 'As soon as this all dies down, she'll be gone. But she stays for now.'

Spence just nodded, looked across at the girl. 'Rodge has spoken.' he said. 'Better find you a mop.'

19

SIX DAYS LATER

Maddy's funeral service took place on a Wednesday afternoon. A larger crew than usual had amassed to watch the return of the mourners as they assembled on the piazza, led by Mrs Marsh wearing a black T-shirt and short skirt.

'Pity.' Spence had said on seeing the impromptu wake get under way, the booze flying out of Pandy's shop in the crates it was delivered in and out on to the streets. 'We could have flogged a bagful of tickets to this with a bit more warning.'

Roger knew he was right about that. But Roger felt that Spence's regret was half-hearted, that they shared the feeling this was a privileged show, one for the true connoisseur.

An excited Mason sat down next to Roger, chewing hard. He offered Roger a paper bag of liquorice allsorts, staring intently out over the piazza. 'This is going to be a gift.' he said. 'Maxine, you want to get yourself over here for this.'

She came and joined them, squeezing past three of the stalwarts from Housing who were effectively seconded to the Show on a full-time basis now and who really didn't want to be anywhere else.

They looked down as Mrs Marsh, standing on one of the benches, was giving a brief peroration punctuated by swigs from an unidentified green bottle. She was surrounded by a decent-sized audience, self-consciously respectful at the moment but which Roger could sense the pressure building up inside. With his well-honed ability to read the group, he predicted serious trouble within the hour. Having a small select group of fellow aficionados to share it with made him look forward to it all the more.

'Wonder what she's saying.' said Maxine.

Spence tutted. 'I've been thinking if there's a way of miking them up down there so we can hear what they're saying.'

'Should be possible.' Mason suggested, offering a sweet. 'You get the right bugging equipment, someone to operate it, should be able to pick it up no bother.'

'Who wants to hear what these knackers have to say?' said Darren from Housing in his druggy drawl. He handed Roger a plastic bag containing a number of different-coloured pills. 'How about one of my allsorts, Rodge?' he asked, making his colleagues snigger. Roger picked out a handful and dropped them into his shirt pocket. 'It's more fun.' Darren went on, 'not knowing why they're acting so barmy.'

'What you reckon, Rodge?' Spence asked him. 'You're the oracle. Sound and pictures? A little son et lumière?'

Roger was undecided. 'I'm not sure if what they say actually matters.' he postulated.

'Exacto.' said Darren.

'They express themselves in actions. That's why we watch them. The reason why they're worth watching is precisely because nobody listens to them.'

'Fucking hell.' said Spence, smirking. 'Hark at Malcolm Muggeridge.'

'Who's Malcolm McGridge?'

Maddy looked self-conscious as all eyes turned towards her. She leaned heavily on the brush she was holding, still favouring her good leg although the plaster was off the other one and Dr Gilbert had declared it on the mend.

'Never heard of him.' she added sheepishly.

Maxine pointed to a vague area on the floor near where Maddy was standing. 'Missed a bit.' she told her.

'Fuck off.' was the response.

'Ooh, feisty.' laughed Maxine. 'Not bad for a dead girl.'

'You want to take a break?' Roger asked her. 'Come and sit down.' he added, not without a glance across at Spence, who nodded.

'Yeah, sure.' he said, budging one seat along to make room. 'After all, it *is* your funeral.'

She sat down next to Roger. When Mason offered his bag of sweets, she took out four and shoved them all into her gob. Chewing fast, she still offered Roger a little smile of authentic pleasure as she sat and watched the embryonic civil disobedience taking place below in her honour.

Preparations for Maddy's funeral had been quickly made. The third floor had heard about it only that same morning, with Roger already wondering at the unnatural amount of activity around the fringes of the piazza. A tip-off from one of Spence's journalist mates with an ear to police radio told them that a dream the night before had convinced Mrs Marsh that Maddy was dead and she wanted a service to be held immediately in line with some idiosyncratic religious beliefs. Any official opposition to the idea had been met with hysterical threats of self-harm. Only the balm of ritual would suffice. The nearest church would apparently do and, with the bereaved mother's denomination unclear except for the fact that she didn't want a woman priest, in stepped the Reverend Malzeard, known for his sympathy for the needs of the working-class community in his parish, to offer his services.

'The turbulent priest' and 'that fucking lefty' was how Fitch had variously described him during the early days of the ASBU, when certain notorious ratboys from the Harlech Estate had sought sanctuary in his church-cum-drop-in injection clinic.

Roger had watched the local lunchtime news as pictures of the service were shown, including shots of a coffin bearing a giant wreath spelling out the word MADZ and Mrs Marsh, ruddy-cheeked and red-eyed, propped up by well-wishers, many of whom had joined her in sporting oversized badges on their coats depicting a younger Maddy at the seaside, a 99 ice cream in one hand and a hot dog in the other.

As they watched now, Mrs Marsh's bearing had temporarily changed as, after her speech, she had re-immersed herself in the crowd and, swaying from side to side, arms around two of her neighbours, she was prominent in some uncompromising community singing, exhorting those who weren't joining in to do so immediately.

'She's loving it.' Maddy said. 'She's never this happy.'

'See, if we had microphones, we'd know what they were singing.' said Spence.

'It's Robbie Williams.' said Maddy quietly.

'How do you know?'

'It's always Robbie Williams. That's "Let Me Entertain You" they're at now.'

'Figures.' said Mason. 'He's always top of the ratbag hit parade.'

Maddy looked back at him.

'No offence.' he said.

'Not bothered.' she replied.

At the edges of the group, the high spirits had spilled over into a disturbance with a camera crew who wanted some pictures of the wake. The watchers on the third floor winced as the sound man took a nasty shot to the head with his own boom, his cameraman dragging him out one-handed before they were chased off. Meanwhile, someone had spoken out of turn to the grieving mother, who was now being restrained from an offensive response, her teeth bared like a crazed dog.

'Here we go.' said Mason, rubbing his hands together. ''S not a proper wake until something kicks off.'

Spence had business concerns. 'We don't want them burning themselves out too early. We've got a houseful of punters tonight, remember.'

'Wouldn't worry about it. It's a special occasion. They're in festival mood.' Mason tousled Maddy's hair. 'Must make you feel special.' he suggested.

Spence leaned across to Roger, spoke low. 'There's something I need to tell you.'

'What's that?'

Spence tried to cough a little rattle in his throat. 'I had a phone call this morning. From Spain.'

'Oh yeah?'

'It was from McNally.'

It took a moment for Roger to register the name of the city's crime supremo.

'What? He just rang you up?'

'It wasn't a total surprise.'

'What you mean?'

Spence looked rueful. 'Spalding…Spalding works for him now. He's been casing us out on McNally's behalf.'

'At least that explains why you were arse-licking the fat bastard.'

'Not my idea of a good time, believe me.'

Roger remembered the 'coincidental' meeting at the magistrates' court. 'How'd they get on to us?'

'Can't be sure, but I'm guessing Johnny couldn't keep his mouth shut.'

Roger exhaled. 'So what did he want?'

'He made us a…proposal.'

Roger gave him a look. 'This is not good, is it?'

Spence tightened his mouth, widened his eyes. 'He wants us to give him a monopoly on the drugs action.'

'Where?'

'Up here. And down there.'

'How can we do that? This lot could find a bag of pills in the Sahara. You told him we didn't have anything to do with it, right?'

Spence flapped his lips.

'I could have told him that. But we both would have known it wasn't true.'

'Sorry. You lost me.'

'We had to have some control, make sure enough stuff was getting through to the knackers.'

'You've been supplying?' asked Roger.

'I should have told you.' admitted Spence. 'It was a business decision.'

Roger wondered how much money Spence was making on this little sideline. More to the point, why hadn't he given Roger any freebies?

'So what you going to do?'

'I'm prepared to negotiate on the narcs. But there's something else.'

'What?'

'The drugs thing I've been talking to with Spalding. I thought I was getting somewhere. That's why I didn't mention it to you.'

'So what's the other thing?'

'We've just been offered protection. McNally wants a cut of what we're making from the Show.'

Roger's eyes danced. 'How much?'

'Half.'

'Half?'

'Fifty per cent. He wants fifty per cent of our hard-earned money.' Spence allowed himself a cold snigger. 'And he can't even be bothered to leave his granny flat in Tenerife to come and ask.'

'But half? They have to be joking.'

'I have to say I didn't get the impression that he was joking. There wasn't much of a jokey atmosphere.'

'But half's crazy. It's ridiculous.'

Spence was silent, thoughtful.

'So you think we should pay him?' Roger asked him.

'Of course I fucking don't.' Spence widened his eyes philosophically. 'But look, this was bound to happen at some point.'

'Why?' Roger hissed. 'Why was it bound to happen? You had to go too far. You had to make it too big. Now we're fucked, way out of our depth.'

Spence took offence. 'Never say that. You never say that to me. You have no idea what my depth is.'

'Do you?'

Spence smirked. 'No, but we're going to find out.' His eyes twinkled with amusement. 'Carlo McNally. Fuck him. I mean, anyone who has to employ that turd Spalding can't be up to much. We'll be OK. Don't sweat it.'

'What are we going to do?'

'Nothing. We'll beef up the security. Let him make his move.'

But Roger remembered their conversation on the barge when Spence had first seen Johnny Odom trundle into view. The fear of McNally had been writ large across his face. Roger knew that it was the insulating influence of the third floor, where anything seemed possible, that encouraged Spence's bravado. He was increasingly aware of the two worlds that existed within and without its confines.

'Spalding.' repeated Spence contemptuously. 'You're right. Shouldn't have lowered myself to dealing with him.' He shivered. 'Sick fucking perv. He's only a rung up the ladder from that…'

He stopped, suddenly possessed by a thought. 'Oh, oh.' he said to himself, then clasped the flat of his hand to his forehead. 'Been staring me in the face. Right in the bloody face.'

He stood up and stepped over Roger's and Maddy's legs to get out, tapping Darren on the thigh as he passed.

'Don't go away.' he told him. 'Just thought of something.'

'Wot? Wot?' giggled Darren.

'Just wait.' said Spence, picking out a number from his mobile's registry. 'I can't believe I hadn't thought of this before This would be…Hey, it's Spence…'

He moved quickly away to the back of the room, speaking low but excitedly to whoever was at the other end. Roger assumed, feared even, another of the 'spectaculars' that Spence was convinced their paying public demanded. In creating the expectation, though, Roger thought there was a law of diminishing returns. The Show itself was the draw, not the creation of greater and greater sideshows. Plus the fact that he couldn't even think of where Spence could go next.

There was something else nagging at him. He'd made a rare excursion out the night before to reluctantly escort a VIP, some soap actor Roger had never heard of. It was on the journey back that Roger noticed Norman wasn't bothering to cut the engines any more. And the babble of the arriving guests, most of them up on deck, necking back the booze and shouting each other down…there was no way they wouldn't hear them on the estate…

Spence drifted back to the window slowly, phone still pressed to his ear, an expansive grin wrapped across his features.

'No…I really appreciate that…Yeah, so what?…Next week at the earliest? That would be huge, massive…Sure, you're on the guest list that night, no problem…and the missus as well, of course, on the house. And free drinks all night, guaranteed. Oh, mate, thanks a million. You've made my day. Cheers, cheers.'

He hung up and threw both fists up in the air.

'What?' Mason wanted to know. 'Who was that?'

'That.' said Spence, still pumped, glancing across at the boys from Housing, 'was Wally Stokes.'

'You're joking?' asked Darren.

'Who's Wally Stokes?' Maxine wanted to know.

'Stokesy.' Darren explained, 'handles the white files. Sensitive housing cases. Intimidation jobs, possible retribution cases, sexual offenders, suspected…' He stopped, looked at Spence wide-eyed. 'You haven't?'

Spence's grin was out of control as he bent double. 'I fucking have.'

'What?' Mason had to know.

'No way.' said Darren.

'Believe it.' said Spence.

'WHAT?'

Spence waited for a moment before spilling it.

'We got Bronsky.'

Mason whooped. Maxine cackled. Darren sat back, whispering the word 'genius'. Roger squeezed the bridge of his nose between forefinger and thumb.

'Who's Bronsky?' Maddy asked him quietly.

'As of today,' Roger answered, 'he's the guy who killed you.'

20

ELEVEN DAYS LATER

Eight thirty and the place was already close to full, the third floor crammed with a sea of bodies. People had wanted to get there early and tonight, with their unexpectedly early congregation at the departure jetty, Spence had decided to start the boat trips over an hour earlier.

Roger sat dead-eyed at the end of the bar, with his back to the window. He felt self-conscious in the tuxedo Spence had persuaded him and all the others to wear. 'Big night. Got to look the part.' he'd asserted. Roger was supposed to be keeping an eye on the punters after Spence's suggestion that they stay alert to any troublemakers. But he was unlikely to step in, whatever was happening. There were a couple of stag parties in (a growing market) along with a bunch of nurses on someone's leaving do. Roger couldn't fathom how a bunch of nurses could afford to be there tonight, not after Spence had hiked up the ticket prices on the promise of retributive justice for Bronsky, the reason why tonight was such a 'special'. Big groups were becoming commonplace. The increasing party atmosphere had been a feature of the last few weeks on the third floor. With that and the availability of private rooms, there had been an upsurge in libidinal behaviour among the Show's increasingly varied clientele. A vogue for drunken female nudity was reaching its apotheosis.

The boozing was up too, with the loungey atmosphere having given way to vertical drinking. And the recreational drug use – that went on all the time, effectively unchecked.

So far tonight there hadn't been any trouble but spirits were unquestionably high. Everyone was up for it tonight. The stag parties and the nurses, cackling like banshees at each other's jokes, were making a fair bit of noise, but that was mostly drowned out by the thumping music that had been introduced through the sound system when Mason was off the mike. Roger didn't care for it, thought that with the coloured disco lights that Spence had redirected from the sensory room at a council-run playgroup made the place look like a shitty nightclub. At least it spared him having to do much talking. Lee took an occasional break from getting in the way behind the bar to come and stand next to him, pushing her body to him and nibbling at his ear while he largely ignored her. Every few minutes Maddy came by as well, back from another tour of the room, collecting glasses.

Roger felt the buzz from his last line of cocaine start to fade. Hadn't lasted long. Getting shorter every time. He stepped off his high stool and started to swerve through the party towards his room. Halfway out he bumped into Spence, wearing his tuxedo with ease but still a bundle of energy, eyes flashing, a film of sweat catching the light on his forehead.

Spence had had a few drinks but he was high on the Show, high on it all. He grabbed Roger by the shoulders and embraced him.

'We did it.' he said. 'This, what we've done here. This is

really something, aye?'

'Yeah.'

'You know.' Spence said, shouting over Roger's shoulder so he could be heard better. 'I never really thanked you for bringing this to me.'

'You don't have to.'

Spence shook his head, got serious. 'No, really. Thanks, Rodge. Thanks for seeing what there was here.' He pointed to the throng. 'Everyone I talk to, everyone who comes here, I tell them, all of them, that it was your idea. People respect you, man.'

Roger looked at him. Despite everything else, he felt an overwhelming sense of emotion towards this man, this friend, an uncontrolled sentimentality which threatened to buckle him.

Spence surveyed the scene. 'Fucking hell. We're going to have to go some to top this.'

Roger smiled quickly, recovered himself. He wanted another line badly. 'Reckon so.'

'This is like a full stop, a punctuation point, you know what I mean?'

Roger pretended he did with a nod.

'Need to come up with something new. Got any ideas?'

'What?'

'Got any ideas? You know, after this. We have to take it up to another level.'

Roger made an exaggerated face and shrugged. 'I'll think about it.' he shouted, trying to get past.

'Where you going?' Spence wanted to know.

'Just popping out. Back in a sec.'

Roger took a couple of steps before he felt Spence jab him twice between the shoulder blades. He turned back.

'By the way.' Spence wanted to know. 'You seen Odom?'

Roger couldn't quite hear. Spence pointed to his mouth

and repeated the question slowly. Roger shook his head.

'No. I saw him around earlier. Why?'

'I like to know where he is, that's all. Get back quick. There's some people I want you to meet. We got the celebs in tonight big time.'

Roger didn't ask who. Not wanting to share his gear with anyone, he sneaked out to his room and did three lines, one and a half for each nostril. When he re-emerged, he had the answer to Spence's question. Out in the corridor was Odom, moving back and forth in his chair with tiny movements of the wheels as he faced Maddy, who was standing with her back pressed to the wall, arms folded, hands lost inside the sleeves of the outsize cardigan Roger had given her. They were chatting quietly, with something Odom had just said making her half-smile coyly. He offered her the cigarette that was smouldering in one of his fingerless leather gloves. She took it, taking a draw just as she heard Roger shut the door to his room behind him. He approached and stopped next to the two of them. Odom continued his mini-rolls back and forth as Roger stood, momentarily unable to speak as the cocaine bit into him.

'I was just saying.' Odom said, still looking at Maddy. 'Just saying, she's got her whole life ahead of her. Makes you jealous, doesn't it?'

Roger tried to answer but it came as a cough.

'Makes me jealous, anyway.' Johnny went on. 'Makes a tired old fart like me jealous. Everything in front of you, everything waiting for you.'

'Should you be smoking?' Roger asked Maddy. Cocaine, he knew, had the effect of making him more self-righteous than normal.

'One puff won't hurt.' said Johnny, winking at her. She laughed at the word 'puff', took a perfunctory drag on the cigarette and gave it back to Odom, who put it to his own mouth slowly, breathing hard through his nose.

'All them experiences.' he said, laying on his Civic Radio growl now. 'All those sensations, all those tastes. Try everything.' he urged her. 'Try it all.'

She nodded. 'That's what I want to do.' she said. 'I'm not afraid.'

'Good.' purred Odom. 'Life's a journey. Uncle Johnny can be your guide, if you want...'

Roger checked back in.

'Glasses need collecting.' he told her. She left, giving him a look, one he recognised from Beth. From another life he might have had, some time in the past.

'She's just a kid.' Roger said as Johnny watched her go.

'We were kids once too.' Odom pointed out. 'And we found the way we wanted to go. Shouldn't hog it all for yourself. You have to be generous.' He paused, considered his next comment. 'Something your man Spence needs to understand.'

'Like how?'

'Like knowing when to open his business up to interested parties.'

'You're talking about McNally?'

'I'm talking about doing the sensible thing. The right thing.'

'The right thing?'

'Right for the circumstances.'

'What circumstances? He wants half the business. You put him on to us, didn't you? You can't keep your mouth shut and the next thing he wants half our fucking business.'

'I hope you're not blaming me. I'd take offence if I thought you were blaming me.'

'You brought him here.' Roger repeated.

'He's impressed with what you're doing here. Not an easy man to impress, I should add. You've made a good friend there.' he told him. 'Keep on the right side of old Carlo and you're doing all right. Take it from Johnny.'

'What did you fucking tell him for?'

Odom looked aghast. 'Word of mouth, that's what Spence wanted. That was the currency you quoted, word of mouth. His very words. You've been generous to old Johnny, making him feel comfortable. He's just tried to do a little on your behalf.'

'We don't need him on board. We don't need a fucking associate.'

'That's where I don't agree. That's where Johnny begs to differ.' Odom sighed regretfully. 'Do you really think he wouldn't have cottoned on by himself? I did you a favour. I smoothed the way. I put myself on the line for you. Johnny's the buffer here. You think Carlo normally stops at half? You're getting off lightly.'

'Spence won't go for it. He thinks he can take him on.'

Johnny turned serious.

'He'll listen to you. Roger. Time is running out. Patience is not Carlo's strong suit.' Johnny made a rush at Roger. Roger felt a hand grip him tightly around the wrist. 'Tell Spence to accept terms. Or Carlo will close you down.'

'What you mean, close down?'

Odom's eyes looked up at him, beseechingly.

'I mean the end of the Show. We don't want to see the Show closed down, do we? No more bread and circuses. Come on…'

'Maybe it would be for the best.' said Roger quietly.

Odom allowed himself a growling laugh. 'For you, maybe. You've done well, Roger, my friend. What we talked about before…your progress, it's been good. I can see you're tired of this—' he waved back towards the party '—vicarious pleasure. Watching isn't enough for the likes of us, is it, Roger? What's that line of poetry? "Sooner murder an infant in its cradle than nurse unacted desires." Something like that. Makes you think, doesn't it? You're close now. Follow your bliss, Roger. Don't let…sentiment—' he spat the word out as if it were a mouthful of sour milk '—for that stupid little tart hold you back.'

Roger was swallowed up by a blend of anger and fatigue. 'I don't know what you're talking about.'

'OK, answer me this. What do you see when you look out that window?'

Roger thought about it. 'I see…people having fun.'

'Exactly. They're the winners. They're the free men. Just bread and circuses for everybody else.' Odom set his chair in motion. 'Tell Spence to agree terms. And tell him quick or it'll get messy. I can't hold them off. Not any more.'

Roger went back into the throng and headed for his seat just as Mason jumped back on to his dais and asked for quiet over the PA system.

'OK, ladies and gentlemen. Good to have you along for this very, very special occasion. Are you ready?'

The crowd whooped and cheered but not to their MC's satisfaction.

'ARE YOU READY?'

The crowd screamed and howled their response.

'All right. Let me direct your attention to the second floor of Bax Villas and more precisely to the third door from the left…'

The TV screens erected on brackets around the rooms all flashed into life with a close-up of a blue door with a yellow cross daubed in paint.

'We've marked it, just so you can see it clearly. Ladies and gentlemen, that flat is, as of four o'clock this afternoon, the new residence of Victor Bronsky, a man who needs no introduction…'

The last words were drowned out in a chorus of booing. Roger imagined Bronsky inside the flat, cold and friendless. He felt himself beginning to root for the underdog. The voice in his head telling him he had to go and talk to Spence was getting quieter, drowned out by the baying on the third floor.

There was, Roger supposed, the hope that nobody on the Composers' would realise who they had in their midst. He'd only been dropped in that afternoon, after all. But Spence had been confident that they would cotton quickly, that they would smell him on the wind and the word would spread on the piazza like wildfire. Roger instinctively knew he was right. For some things the *artistes* could just be relied on.

As Mason set about stirring up more frenzy with a brief outline of Bronsky's 'career', Roger ordered himself another drink. He'd have a word with Spence later. As he turned back into the room, two young men were facing him. Roger's first thought was that they might be McNally's men and that his next sensation might be a fist in the face. But they weren't the right type, Roger decided. Closer inspection showed they were bedecked in short-sleeved Hawaiian shirts, clutching bottles of PoundBlaster premium lager. They were the ones looking intimidated at being in his presence.

'You Roger?'

Roger nodded, sniffed back, trying to hoover up any coke dust still lurking on his nose hairs.

'We asked…' one of them said, looking quickly over his shoulder. 'The bloke…'

The other one interjected. 'The bloke we were talking to, he was over there somewhere…'

'…He said you were the person to come and see.'

Roger's eyes danced. 'About what?'

The two glanced at each other.

'We were just saying to this bloke, over there. We were just saying that, you know, rather than just sitting up here, it'd be good to get down there…'

'…Mix it up…'

'…You know?'

'…All our mates would be up for it…'

'…Pay extra, like…'

Roger stared back at them with an intensity that seemed genuinely to frighten them.

'You want to go out on to the piazza?'

They nodded.

'Beyond the glass?'

'That's the idea.'

'You want to be like them?'

The question puzzled the one on the left, who shook his head. 'Nah, mate. We want to kick the shit out of them.'

Roger could only stare and blink. Perhaps they felt they had made an impertinent suggestion, that they were treading on the sensitive toes of a hard-nosed businessman, for they took his silence as an invitation to drift away. In truth, Roger was in a kind of shock. How could something so obvious have passed Spence by? Roger, however, was glad that it had. Instinctively, the idea appalled him. He wanted them left alone down there, uncorrupted.

He was disturbed by the sensation of somebody watching him from down the bar. He glanced across and saw a familiar woman, handbag clutched to her chest, sliding the length of the bar towards him.

'Hello.' she said, pecking him on the cheek in a pointed display of civility that was typical of her. Her hair was different and she looked slimmer, he thought.

'Hi.' Roger replied, pursing his mouth to voice a question that never came.

'So this is where you've been hiding?' she said, sliding on to the stool next to him.

'Yeah. You want a drink?'

Marion noted the preference Roger got at the bar.

'You're something to do with all this?' she asked rhetorically. 'I saw Spence over there. The two of you together?'

'Him mainly.'

'You shouldn't let him take all the credit.'

Roger took a sharp swig of his alcopop and sucked on his teeth. 'Marion, what the hell are you doing here?'

She looked affronted. 'What? My money not good enough for you? I wanted to come.'

'How did you find out about it?'

She shook her head. 'Everybody knows. Everyone at work talks about it.'

'Work?'

Her mouth tightened. 'You don't think I was just going to sit around after you'd left. No.' she said, sipping at a glass of white wine that she was handed. 'You did me a favour. It was going nowhere, let's face it.'

'What work are you doing?'

'SecuroBlast. Insurance sales. I enjoy it.'

'So you're here with people from work?'

'No. Lots of the girls have been. They raved about it. But I came on my own. Wanted to come tonight, so I bought a ticket from someone I know in human resources.'

'But you're still getting my wages from the council, aren't you?'

She smiled thinly, looking around the room, then widened her eyes, dipped slightly on her chair. 'Oh, I'm so excited.' she said.

'By what?'

'I can't wait to see that disgusting man get what's coming to him.'

It took Roger a moment to realise she was referring to Bronsky. He dimly recalled her expressing a view on him in their imagined life together.

'They're probably going to kill him.'

'Good.'

'Isn't that extreme?'

'What do you care? From what I can see, you're making plenty of money out of it.'

This was undeniable.

'So when will it start?' Marion asked.

'What?'

'The entertainment.'

'You mean the lynching?'

'The main event.' she replied, staring at him unimpressed. *We're still married*, he thought. He wondered what she'd say if he suggested they went and got a room.

'Give it time.' he said. 'Most of the headliners haven't come out yet.'

'I hear Wayne Morphy's good value.'

Roger tried not to sound surprised at her knowledge. 'He's a showboater. Lacks nuance.' he told her.

'Who's your favourite?' she asked, her guard dropped.

'No favourites.' he said, draining his bottle and lining up another. 'For me, it's not about personalities. It's about the…you know, the whole thing…'

He felt her hand fall on to his knee.

'The kids are very impressed. You should hear Nick talk about it. He can't wait to come for himself.' The hand gripped his thigh a notch tighter. 'No one's angry with you. Nobody wants to take this away from you. You can come home and still have it.'

He looked intently at her, trying to summon a response. Everything that Marion represented came sharply into focus: family, security, responsibility. Trapped in a swamp of hedonism, they seemed exotic, almost fantastic propositions. From where he was sitting, impossibly dangerous. He preferred the safety of casual sex, the conservatism of extreme drug abuse.

But when, he wondered, was this cocaine going to do anything for him?

Two more hands were on him, this time moving down his chest and stomach. Lee had approached from behind, and as she licked the back of his neck her fingers reached his crotch.

'Who's this, baby?' she asked him, tossing her hair as Marion sat back.

Roger gave Marion a weak smile. 'This is my wife.' he told Lee. 'She wants me to go back home.'

Lee laughed and stared at her rival. 'Why would he want to go back with you? He's got everything he needs right here.'

Roger blinked, waiting for Marion to respond, hoping she'd hit back with something good. He decided he quite fancied seeing the fur fly.

'You're not really with this little scrubber?' she asked Roger.

'Her name's Lee.' Roger said.

'Yeah.' said Lee, 'so go fuck yourself.'

Roger quickly unwrapped himself from her arms and grabbed her hard by the wrists, digging his thumbs in to make it hurt.

'That's my wife you're talking to. More respect. Apologise.'

Lee set her mouth tight. Marion looked indulgent. 'Don't worry. I understand. It must be flattering. But you'll get tired of her, Roger.'

'Wasn't tired last night.' hissed Lee. 'Fucked all night.' she lied. Hydraulically assisted by a gobful of Viagra, Roger had expended himself quickly into her mouth and fallen asleep in a chair. But he chose not to contradict her.

Marion held on to a mask of detached sophistication.

'Men have needs, I understand that. I realise that I need to be a bit more open-minded. I mean.' she said, recrossing her legs, 'it's quite normal on the Continent for happily married men to go with prostitutes. It's fine by me.'

'Tell her not to call me a prostitute.' snarled Lee, but Roger waved her complaints away.

'Semantics.' he said, then readdressed Marion. 'So Lee could come and live with us?' Roger laughed.

'I don't know.' answered Marion with admirable calm. 'Is she house-trained?'

Roger experienced a sudden, sharp visualisation of himself in a threesome with Lee and Marion. Was it possible to draw everybody down into the vortex with him? That was his democratic urge.

'Why don't you come and stay here instead?' he asked, prompted by the thought. 'And the kids.' he added, suddenly excited by the prospect. He leaned forward and took his turn to squeeze Marion's leg, high above the knee. 'It'll be a laugh.'

Roger had wanted to see what Lee's reaction would be, whether he could actually manufacture a fight between them, but they were sidetracked by a key change in Mason's voice over the loudspeakers.

'OK, I think we're starting to see some action here. Looks as if tonight's main event is about to get under way. Remember, for those who can't get a proper view, the action will be relayed on the giant screen…'

Roger glanced across to see a group of residents, most of whom he recognised instantly, moving at unusual speed along the balcony below Bronsky's level and beginning their ascent up the stairs at the far end towards him.

As usual, Mason was on the ball with his facts.

'…OK, leading the way with the shaved head and the England shirt circa 1990 is Melvin, or Mel, Cullen. Interestingly, for a man outraged at the presence of a paedophile on the estate, Mel has two convictions for sex with underage girls…'

Marion got off her stool. 'I'm going to get a better view.' she said. 'That's what I came for.' she added, as if in defence of her action. But she stood for a moment, waiting for something. At that moment Roger saw another presence sailing against the tide of bodies. It was Spence, hand stretched behind him as he pulled someone along.

Outside, the first courageous souls with sledgehammers had started attacking the door of Bronsky's abode.

'Rodge.' shouted Spence over the noise. 'I got someone here who wanted to…' He stopped, clocked the gathering. 'Marion?' he said.

'Spence.' replied Marion, clutching her handbag tighter to her chest.

'What are you…?'

'Bought a ticket, like everybody else.' she snapped.

'You should have said.' Spence chided her. 'You could have come for nothing, isn't that right, Rodge?'

But Roger was looking at the girl on Spence's arm. Spence drew her forward.

'There's someone here who wanted to meet you.'

Roger got off his chair and wiped his hand across the backside of his trousers before taking the outstretched hand of the young woman. She had brown hair with blonde tints, unnaturally straight, cascading down bare shoulders. She wore a white halter top (Roger thrilling at the sight of a red bra strap) and a short leather skirt which tantalisingly just failed to meet the tops of a pair of long boots. Roger took a moment to explore the familiar face carefully. He knew those dark, provocative eyes well and the loose, full mouth, lazily chewing gum. Her heavy layering of make-up had cracked a little around her nose and the corners of her tight, sneering mouth. A coarse perfume surrounded her.

Lorraine from CostBlast. In the flesh, a thousand times

more magnificent than he could ever have dreamed.

'Hi.' he said. 'It's an honour to have you here.'

She made no response other than to thrust out a hip, giving Lee and Marion a cursory glance.

'How long you in town?' he asked.

'Just the night.' she said.

'Work?' he asked.

She nodded. 'Personal appearance at the PoundBlaster Centre. Me and Alex.' She gestured further down the bar to where a lean, suited man Roger recognised from the channel was standing, his head thrown back in laughter as one of the nurses' party lifted her T-shirt and shook her sizeable breasts at him.

When he looked back, Lorraine had taken a step towards him. She leaned to speak conspiratorially into his ear. 'I heard you were the guy to talk to if I wanted a party.'

Roger leaned further in. 'How do you mean?'

He felt her hand brush his elbow, liquefying him with lust.

'I want to get high, babes. I heard you were pilled up. How about you and me go and have some private fun?'

She took him by the hand, suggesting that he lead the way.

Roger cast his eye around.

Lee looking at him.

Marion looking at him.

Behind the bar, Maddy looking at him.

Roger took a deep breath, realised this was a test. Each of them, for their own selfish reasons, wanted him to stay, but he was being summoned by a force greater than they could understand. To reject Lee, to humiliate Marion, to disappoint Maddy, these were the petty considerations that were supposed to hold him back from taking this, his greatest possible pleasure, the ultimate expression of his own abandonment to freedom.

'I'd like that.' he told Lorraine, as the first Molotov cocktail went crashing through Bronsky's window.

He caught Spence's eye as he passed. He paused for a moment, wondering whether he should tell him what Odom had said about the McNallys. Now didn't seem like the right time. He'd tell him later. And besides, Roger felt, consummation with CostBlast Lorraine and his transformation would be complete. As they left, Roger saw Odom hovering near the door. Johnny watched them go, offered a small nod of encouragement.

On the big screen, they had kicked in the door to Bronsky's flat.

There didn't need to be a Show any more.

They held hands to the door of his room. He opened the door and led her in.

She followed him around to the side of the bed, where he sat down, letting her stand over him. Looking up at her, Roger let a tear slide from the corner of his eye.

'What'sa matter, hun?' she asked, stroking his head once.

'Thank you.' he said.

''S OK.' she said, as if she really understood. 'So what you got for me?'

He reached out and opened the top drawer to the cabinet. They looked down at the contents, the hundreds of pills – speed, Valium, uppers, downers, ecstasy, Viagra – all rolling freely among the slabs of dope, the bags of cocaine and the smaller wraps of crack he'd been saving for the right moment.

This was evidently the right moment.

'Quite a sweetshop.' she said, coming to sit on his knee.

'What do you want to try?' he asked.

'Everything.' she replied, taking off her top and unclasping her bra. Her breasts sprang forward. Noticing one was larger than the other, Roger cupped them gently, felt the scarring underneath where she had been operated on for their enhancement, traced the stretchmarks heading towards her armpits with his fingertips.

'You like them?' she asked.

He nodded. 'Perfect. Just perfect.'

INTERMEZZO

21

Noise
Noises
Shouting
Screaming
Outside
Awake
Pills
Pills everywhere
Lorraine
Cold
Head. Splitting
Shouting
Bat
Get bat
Outside
Screaming
Smoke
People
Running
Panic
Head
Splitting

Running
Lights
Disco lights
Red
Green
Panic
Lights
Big screen
Fire!
Smoke
Spence
Two of them
Spence held
Spence's face
Smack!
Spence down
Spence down!
Kicking
Head
Disco lights
Spalding
Head
Spence
Spence's head
Kicked in
Disco lights
Green
Blue
Red
Bat
Spalding
Bat
Thwack
Thwack

Spalding
Down
Thwack
Thwack
Thwack
Bone
Blood
Thwack
Spence
Still
Disco lights
Red
Green
Big screen
Fire
Smoke
Scream
Maddy!
Running
Scream
Door
Maddy!!
No!!
Bat
Bat
Bat
Bat
Bat
Bat
Bat
Bat
Bat

PART THREE

22

'And tell me, have you fully costed this proposal?'

'What do you mean, costed?' asked Roger, putting his hands to his head. 'I don't understand what you mean.' He screwed his eyes shut and tried to calm himself. 'I'm sorry, what does that mean?'

Councillor Peter Pease looked up at him, as if in dispute with a foreign waiter. 'To demolish a building costs money. It is not.' he added, licking his lips, 'an act of charity. It requires the consideration of highly skilled professionals, all of whom are fully insured against any potential claims made against them. Full risk assessments must be undertaken and analysed. Full business plans must be drafted, including the preparation of complete *costings*, incorporating an additional percentage for unforeseen contingencies. It really is quite simple.'

'But there were plans in place. You were going to knock it down anyway.'

'Were we?'

'Yes. DemoRent were going to flatten it. We had it called off.'

'Called off? How were you…?' asked Pease, unable to hide his disdain.

Roger talked fast. 'We moved the gypsies in. We paid the

gypsies to come on site so the demolition was impossible. People we knew in Housing went along with it. They were busing tenants in to condemned housing stock. Everyone was in on it.'

Pease sat back in his chair.

'Are you intimating corruption among council employees?'

'Not corruption. I don't know what you'd...It was a business venture.' he suggested, trying to plead to Pease's apparent soft spot. 'We were all showing our initiative.' He sat down, made an effort to tap into the stream of the councillor's discourse. 'Unfortunately, we made one or two business decisions which proved to be counter to the general...erm...the general good of the business model.'

'What kind of business do you mean?'

Roger rolled his head back, blinked a few times. 'Entertainment. Public entertainment.'

'Unlicensed?'

Now Roger nodded, his whole body going up and down with his head. 'Yes, yes, unlicensed. The unlicensed fucking display of antisocial behaviour.'

The question was there in the slight furrowing of Pease's brow.

'We sold tickets, people came to watch.'

'Watch who?'

'The plebs. We sold tickets, people came to watch the fucking chavs smash everything up.'

'Which people?'

'Everybody. Everybody in the town who wasn't smashing stuff was watching them do it.' He looked down at himself. 'I'm covered in fucking blood here. I'm soaked in blood. Everybody. My wife showed up, can you believe that? I haven't seen her for months and she turns up at the Show, wanting to see Bronsky get it. She paid five hundred quid to watch them kick the shit out of an old man. Like it was a Barbra

Streisand concert.'

Roger looked off into the corner of the room as a giant wave of fatigue threatened to flatten him. 'Your secretary.' he said to Pease, lazily throwing a thumb over his shoulder. 'Out there. She'll tell you. She came, more than once. I thought I recognised her. Last time I saw her she was stark naked, dancing on a table for a free drink.' He spied a two-seater settee at the back of the room, a small coffee table in front of it. 'I could really do with a kip. You don't mind if I…?'

Pease agreed with a minimalist gesture. As Roger laid down his head, he heard the councillor switch on the intercom on his desk.

'Janet, would you be good enough to come in for a moment?'

23

When he woke, Roger wasn't in Pease's office any more. He wasn't covered in blood either. He was in bed, under a sheet and blanket with a short-sleeved smock on. The room was plainly decorated in white paint, but he noticed there were a few patches where a second coat had been applied sloppily.

Council painters, he thought. *I'm on council property*.

From his prone position, he could see nothing but grey, darkening sky through the window. After a few minutes of groggy wakefulness, he heard the sound of glass smashing and a lazy clap of footsteps on concrete paving.

He knew he was back on the Composers'.

In the room with him, next to the door, sat a large man in a white shirt and black trousers doing a puzzle in a magazine. Roger didn't recognise him. He lay and watched for a while, trying to establish what might be going on until he instinctively scratched an itch on his chin. The sound of his nail scraping against stubble alerted the seated man to his consciousness.

'What do you know?' he asked rhetorically. 'It's alive.'

He stood up, opened the door and shouted a general message outside.

'He's awake!' He turned back to Roger. 'They'll be here in a minute. You want a glass of water or something?'

'Anything stronger?' Roger asked, pulling himself up into an approximation of a sitting position. The man just returned to his seat, shaking his head softly with amusement.

After a few moments there were two brisk taps on the door and it opened. In marched a small, bespectacled man Roger dimly recognised.

'Hello, Mr Merrion.' he said briskly, Roger aware that he didn't want to look him directly in the eye. 'How are you feeling?' he asked, glancing at a chart he had collected from the end of the bed.

'I don't know. Still tired.'

'That's not altogether surprising. You've been under sedation for a few days. You were in quite a nervous state after the…events.'

'Why am I back here? This place isn't safe.'

The doctor – Roger thought he might be a doctor – smiled indulgently. 'It's safe, believe me. As safe as anywhere right now. And the facilities here are quite adequate. Better than adequate, in fact. You'd be surprised.'

Roger tried to pull himself higher. 'Where's Maddy?' he wanted to know.

The doctor inhaled hard through his nose. 'She's here. She's around.'

Roger remembered. He was the doctor who'd fixed her leg. Couldn't remember his name right now.

'Is she all right?'

'Seems fine.'

'I want to see her.'

The doctor thought about it. 'I think that could be arranged.'

'What about Spence?'

'He won't be popping in.'

'How is he?'

'Coma.' the doctor told him, starting to pick something out

of his teeth. 'Persistent.'

'What are his chances?'

The doctor shrugged. 'He may live to fight another day. Let's hope so, aye?'

Roger fell silent while the doctor made a couple of notes. He tried to remember.

'What about—' Roger dropped his voice so that the man at the door (why did they need a man on the door?) couldn't hear '—what about the Show? You know about the Show, right?'

The doctor finally looked him in the eye and nodded.

'It couldn't go on.' said Roger. 'We were in trouble. It had to come to an end.'

'All good things…' mused the doctor.

'Yeah.'

The doctor stood up. 'It's all in hand.' he said. 'You did the right thing. Everything's going to be fine.'

'But Spence. In a coma, you say?'

The doctor gave a tight smile. 'I'll let them know you're awake.'

A few minutes later Maddy slipped in, carrying a couple of cans bearing the PoundBlaster logo.

'Hey. You woke up.' As if it was a surprise.

'Yeah.'

She looked down at his hand, resting on the bed. 'And…thanks.' she added, sipping her can and looking down.

Roger had to blink hard a couple of times. He felt strange. 'For what?'

Her eyes lifted to look at him.

'Thanks?' he reminded her. 'What for? Thanks for what?'

She looked worried for a moment, her mouth turned down in what might have been confusion or, equally likely, pity. 'For helping me.' she said.

Roger tried sitting up. 'Maybe you'd have been better off if you'd never come here.'

She looked upset. 'I like it here.'

'Well, don't get too comfortable. It's not going to last, thank God.'

The effort of straightening himself was too much and he began to feel dizzy and fell back on his pillows with a groan. Maddy pushed the spare can she had towards him.

'Try some of this.'

'What is it?'

'It's new.'

Roger inspected the can. Life*Blast!* declared the logo on the front, adding that whatever was inside contained essence of guarana. With an effort, he ripped the tab off and took a drink. It was warm and sweet, hard to swallow. He licked his bottom lip, where a few drops were threatening to set in a hard film.

'Not like it?' she asked.

'I think I'd rather just have a glass of water.'

'I'm like totally addicted to it.' she said. 'There's loads going. We've got crates of it. And boxes of Blast Bars.' she added, producing a couple of the gaudily wrapped products and putting them at his bedside. 'You can just help yourself. It's lush.'

Roger put this down to youthful exaggeration. He shut his eyes just as there was a sound of the door opening again.

'If you'd be so kind…' said a voice he knew, directed at Maddy.

'All right.' she answered petulantly. 'You want to take a chill pill, mate,' she muttered, the chair beneath her scraping on the floor as she stood up. Roger felt a soft pressure on his forehead, followed by a certain dry stickiness on separation. Maddy had just kissed him.

'He's tired.' he heard her say. 'So don't…'

The door closed. Roger sensed two presences in the room.

Reluctantly he opened his eyes. Councillor Peter Pease stood at the end of the bed, inspecting him. Dr Gilbert was back and in motion, moving around the side of the bed to remove the PoundBlaster goods.

'Best keep you off this stuff for the minute.' He smiled indulgently. 'We need to regularise your metabolism a bit.' He leaned across the bed and put a finger to each of Roger's cheeks in turn, pulling down the skin to inspect his eyes. Apparently satisfied, he seized his arm by the wrist and pushed in a thumb to check his pulse.

Roger couldn't help imagining Spence's response at the sight of Pease standing inside Goossens, the house that they'd built, but for Roger it represented the ultimate sense of release, even if the councillor's close inspection of him was unnerving.

'So you've seen for yourself.' Roger said. 'I wasn't lying.'

'Evidently not.' Pease glanced across at the doctor as he stood back. 'Well?'

'Should be OK. Not for too long, though. An hour, maximum.'

Pease nodded. 'I'd like you to get dressed…if you feel able.' he said, the last sentiment unconvincingly tagged on. 'There's a meeting in progress. You may find it of interest.'

He gestured to a pile of clothes Roger recognised as his own, salvaged from the wardrobe strewn across the floor of his fourth-floor flat. Cleaned and pressed as well, he noticed as he donned them over his cold, almost translucent skin. Roger noticed how thin he had become.

He ventured out into the corridor, where Mason and Maxine were waiting for him, standing on either side of the door, both leaning tight to the wall.

'Rodge.' Mason splurted, quickly squatting to put his can of Life*Blast!* on the floor before standing again to give Roger an embrace. 'How are you, mate?'

Roger had to think about it. 'I'm all right.' he said, extracting himself. Maxine took a step towards him but no more. She didn't really do personal contact unless it amounted to a collision. 'You two still here? What you doing here?'

They shared a look.

'Just clinging on.' said Mason, with a tight smile. Maxine scratched her chin.

'You heard about Spence?' he asked them.

'Yeah. We knew.'

'I had to tell Pease.' he said, swallowing hard. 'There wasn't anything else to do. I was the one who told him to demolish it. We couldn't carry on, not without Spence. You understand that?'

Mason slapped him on the shoulder, nodding a furrowed brow.

'Rodge, you don't have to explain yourself to us. It'll all work out for the best. Come on.' he went on, leaning against Roger to lead him towards the stairwell. 'We'll take you to your meeting.'

Roger took the hint and led them along the corridor to the stairs, his continuing sense of dizziness causing him to reach for the banister as he took the first step down.

'Rodge.'

'Huh?'

Roger looked to see Mason's finger pointing skywards.

'It's upstairs. We're on the second here.'

Roger stared at him for a second. Things weren't quite adding up but it was hard to concentrate when his mouth was so dry. Clapping his lips together a few times in an attempt to get some saliva going, he started to climb.

They were waiting for him as he stepped on to the third floor, seated round a large oval table only a few feet from the window. Roger knew most of them, knew who they were at least.

Pease was alone in being on his feet, peering out on to the piazza with a fascination Roger was all too familiar with before turning as he came in and gesturing to the other empty chair. As he slowly approached, Roger's eye was caught by the large pile of crates and boxes near the canteen, all bearing the PoundBlaster logo. Roger could make out the forms inside of Life*Blast!* cans and Blast Bars. Those at the table, he noticed as he sat down, were sitting behind bottles of PoundBlaster Luxury Table Water, with a choice of still or gently sparkling.

Roger looked around the table. Beside Pease sat the doctor. Flanking him on the other side was a copper in uniform, the deputy chief constable who Roger recognised from the telly when Maddy had gone missing. He gave Roger a strongly disapproving look. Elsewhere, under an eruption of red hair, a giant scarf exuding ethnic chic wrapped repeatedly around her neck until it resembled a brace, there was Maggie Roach, the feared head of Social Services in the local authority. She eyed Roger inscrutably. Next to her was Alan Uddin, chief of Housing for the entire council, who had once worked with Roger and Spence at the lower levels before moving on to greater things. As ever, he radiated nervous energy, avoiding eye contact, hunched forward over the desk, momentarily dropping his pen from its routine of note-making to scratch both his upper arms at the same time. Altogether more calm was a white-haired man with a haughty disposition and a cold wolf-like stare as he looked into the space ahead of him, hands resting on his lap. Roger, even in his hazy state, instinctively knew this was the Reverend Huw Malzeard, no less. The dog collar probably gave it away as well.

The big guns, thought Roger, although he didn't know who the suit was, pointedly flipping through his copy of the document they all had in front of them, clearly having given up trying to engage the reverend in polite conversation. He was probably a big gun too, which made it all the stranger that the last person at the table, who Roger had seen immediately, was present. But there he was, sitting directly opposite him, Roger aware of the intensity of his gaze right at him, which he fought not to meet.

Fitch. For the first time, Roger felt ashamed.

Pease started talking. 'I'm pleased to say that Mr Merrion is well enough to join us for this part of the proceedings. Now that we've all had ample time to absorb the contents of the dossiers...'

Pease and his fucking dossiers, thought Roger, looking down at the one they had put where he was sitting. Carefully formatted. Bound and covered. He remembered the business plan discussion they'd had in his office. Christ, all you needed was a wrecking ball and the will to get it done. Still, Roger consoled himself, whatever it took was worth it. He glanced down at the cover, where a gap in the leather-effect plastic allowed him to see the title:

GOOSSENS HOUSE PROJECT – INITIAL BUSINESS PLAN

'...and you've heard the presentations from myself and Mr Hendrick.' Pease went on, gesturing towards the previously anonymous suit, who looked up with a stagy smile. 'I'd be grateful for your submissions, perhaps starting with you, deputy chief constable.'

'Well, thank you, Mr Chair. After consultation with my colleagues and superiors and based on the guarantees made by you and Mr Hendrick, I've been given the authority to notify the group collected here today that we consider this proposal to be—' He paused a moment and glanced around. Roger detected a slight increase of tension in the room. '—practically operable from a law-and-order standpoint...'

The tension in the room was held as the others glanced

among themselves, even the reverend cocking an eyebrow in the direction of Maggie Roach, who scratched a quick note with her fountain pen. Only Fitch responded overtly, letting a hiss of breath out through his teeth. Roger sneaked a quick look at his boss, still finding it strange that Fitch was even there. As if the whole thing wasn't strange enough, like a bad dream...

The copper was still going...

'...Our own figures show as highly significant the percentage of police time that antisocial behaviour, erm, takes. Plus the associated costs. To actually ring-fence that obligation in the way described would be, erm, a good thing. Therefore, with the additional investment from Mr Hendrick's company, we think we can find the necessary manpower to operate what the proposal calls for.'

'So if I can just interrupt.' butted in Pease. 'You accept the principle of value in this proposal?'

The policeman nodded. 'In principle, that would be a yes. Although a full costing—'

'Of course.' agreed Pease, asserting an article of faith.

'We're assuming that the cost of cordoning off the area—'

'Covered as part of the initiative.' Pease assured him. 'Agreed?' he asked Hendrick, who scurried to his papers.

'I think.' the suit said, jutting out his chin and scanning quickly, 'we've factored that in as an exceptional with maintenance included as part of the ongoing costs.'

'Yes, well, that being the case, I don't see us having any objection.'

Roger was having trouble keeping up with this. He allowed himself a guilty look out through the window and on to the piazza. It was a beautiful day outside. The piazza was empty apart from the customary slothful truants lounging around the swings and benches, absorbed in their perpetual cycle of bullying and victimhood. Across in Bax, he saw the remains of

Bronsky's flat, boarded up, the surrounding area blackened like a nasty bruise. Roger wondered for a second whether he had lived or died but the question was extinguished by the sight of activity outside Pandy's shop. The shopkeeper was outside, flanked by a pair of taller men, both wearing suits. Even at a distance, Pandy was all nervous excitement, using expansive gestures to make his point. Turning back towards his shop, he pointed up to show the men the sign over the door declaring it to be Pandy's Handy. They were nodding respectfully at whatever bollocks he was spouting.

He was pulled back into the room by a cry of 'Value' from Pease, looking around the room. 'In my capacity, with my responsibility to the local taxpayer, value has to be the key here. Without value, there is no project.'

Jesus, thought Roger. By the time these knackers have finished, you could have pulled the fucking place down with a teaspoon.

The reverend raised a hand. 'If I might take the opportunity to make a contribution.' he said in a rattling baritone. His mouth movements were minimal but enough for Roger to see the blackened state of his teeth. Easily a forty-a-day man, he surmised, as the reverend took in a deep breath through his nose and, looking into the void ahead of him, began.

'Value is a word with an unfortunately capitalistic overtone. But I, too, am concerned with...value. For a churchman, any ministry has *value*. I feel that my contribution in the terms of this—' he waved down at the dossier with a hint of contempt '—scheme would be *valuable*. Clearly, one has reservations...'

Roger's eyes tightened. *What reservations?* And anyway, what was *he* doing here? Was this consecrated ground or something?

'...The church has a moral responsibility, but it also has a duty to be practical and effect real change in the lives of those who come to it. After much reflection, it is my view that the inhabitants of the estate, both present and future, would be best served by this proposal. The promise of a new church building is not one that anyone in my position can take lightly.'

Roger's face had twisted into a mask of puzzlement. They were going to build a church here now?

'As someone with a particular knowledge of the needs of these people.' the reverend was still going, drawing his hands together and interlocking his fingers while nodding sagely, 'I would be prepared to offer up my own services and take on the challenge of this exceptional ministry.'

The reverend closed his eyes as he finished, allowing the importance of his peroration to sink in. In his enthusiasm, Hendrick had to butt in.

'Don't worry, vicar. We'll make it worth your while.'

The reverend's eyes snapped open, revealing a sulphurous gaze.

Pease pointed towards the only woman on the team. 'Maggie?'

'Look.' she said, letting out a sigh. 'I have enormous respect for the reverend and the work that he does within the community. But you know, platitudes don't pay no rent. What we've got to face up to here.' she huffed, 'is a management issue. Problems on the scale we've got them and make no mistake we got 'em bad I'm talking social exclusion issues subsistence issues domestic violence issues self-esteem issues right across the board we can't just be airbrushing them out I'm working with a straitjacket on and, you know, bringing the mountain to Mohammed isn't so easy with a funding cap let's not kid ourselves I can't just click my little red shoes and take us all back to Kansas…'

Maggie was strong on her pop cultural references. Roger found himself refocusing on Pandy outside, who was being given a clipboard by one of his two companions on the piazza. He made a show of reading it carefully but he was fidgeting, having trouble controlling himself.

Roger put a fingertip on his copy of the dossier and slid it towards himself, idly flipping through it from back to front. The thing was full of Pease's beloved graphics and diagrams. He stopped to look at the significance of one chart where a line crept encouragingly upwards between two sets of parameters. It was entitled *Projected earnings from Goossens site over five-year period using prices as per diagram 5b*. What earnings? he wondered. They were going to charge rent on the land from a church? He turned to the front, saw a list of contents under the main heading.

GOOSSENS HOUSE PROJECT – INITIAL BUSINESS PLAN
1. **Preliminary**
2. **Goossens House – proposal**
3. **Remainder of Composers' Estate – proposal**
4. **Logistical**
5. **PFI contribution**
6. **Timescale**
7. **Conclusion**

He looked outside again. Pandy had got about halfway through the document he was reading before he just flipped straight to the end. He looked up at the two men and shook his head repeatedly. One of them handed him a pen.

Roger turned and let his eyes drift across the chapter entitled *Preliminary*, feeling a twinge of guilt. *Derelict site…trusted council employees…abuse…fraud…unlicensed…*

But they had him sitting here.

He turned the page to the next chapter. *Goossens House – Proposal*.

Maggie was still drivelling on.

'…Clearly I'm going to have issues. Any woman with the scars of the Thatcher junta is going to have issues with this…But, hey, it's Chinatown.' She took a mighty breath. 'My ultimate responsibility is to vulnerable groups. And, in this job, if you can't stand the heat, then, honey, you shouldn't be standing next to the Aga…'

Roger saw that Pandy was signing the last page on the clipboard. When he'd done that, they gave him another one to do the same. Then they let him keep the pen. Clapping him on the back, the two men walked to a black Lexus parked close by. Pandy watched and waved as they did a three-pointer and roared off the estate. Once out of sight, Pandy did something odd.

He fell to his knees and looked up to the clear blue sky. As if he was praying.

With a long, tired blink, Roger started to read the first paragraph of the proposal.

Pease had decided to interrupt Maggie's one-woman show.

'Can I just clarify your position?'

She rolled her eyes, made a flaring motion with her hand. 'You know, I just think it's important that people don't assume that I'm selling out on my commitment.'

Roger screwed his eyes shut and shook his head. He went back to the start of the paragraph.

Pease was losing patience.

'Miss Roach…'

'It's Mrs.'

'Mrs Roach, can you give us a response?'

She dropped her pen with a clatter on the table. 'The drop-in centre's guaranteed?' she wanted to know.

'Guaranteed.' confirmed Pease, seeking back-up from Hendrick, who nodded.

'You saw my staff costings?'

Hendrick nodded again without looking up. 'Covered.' he said.

Maggie looked at the others, her head moving gently from

side to side. 'Then it's wham, bam, thank you, mam. Let's go to w—'

'NO!'

Roger picked up the dossier he had been reading and flung it hard across the table towards Pease, who stood his ground.

'No way.' Roger growled. 'No fucking way.'

The others at the table exchanged meaningful looks.

'You can't agree to this.' he told them. 'No!'

Malzeard addressed Pease. 'He didn't know before you brought him here?'

'I anticipated this kind of response. My intention was to prove how far we had come in developing the proposals. You see, Mr Merrion, that we're quite serious in keeping the operation going, under our own auspices. We're already well advanced. I'm afraid your objection won't alter that.'

'I don't believe this.' Roger muttered. 'You're seriously intending to run it as—' he quoted from what he had just read '—corporate entertainment?'

The suit stood up and moved around the table towards him with a killer smile.

'We're going to make it bigger and better.'

Roger looked at him contemptuously. 'I'm sorry. Just who the fuck are you?'

'Ralph Hendrick.' he said, stepping around the table to offer his hand. 'PoundBlaster Consortium.'

'Eh?'

'We're grateful.' Pease explained, 'to have the support of the PoundBlaster Group in this venture.'

'What's a grocer got to do with it?'

Pease referred him to the oracular dossier, which he flung back at Roger. 'Chapter Five.'

Roger rummaged to open the file.

'PFI?'

'Private Finance Initiative. Mr Hendrick's group have

expressed an interest in helping us to fund the project.'

Roger was struggling. 'Why?' he asked, almost plaintively now.

'We think it's going to be big. We want to be associated with this brand. And it's.' he added, gesturing out to the estate, 'the perfect ready-made testing ground for some of our newer lines.'

Roger looked back at him, wide-eyed.

'We're keen to test brand loyalty among certain socio-economic groups. Everyone's a winner.' said Hendrick with a lopsided grin, gesturing to the boxes of confectionery piled high in the corner. 'Blast Bars. Complimentary, mate.' he added with a wink. 'Fill your boots.'

Roger rubbed his temples. 'You promised me it was coming down. You promised to knock it down.'

'I made no such assurance.' Pease answered. 'It was a possible course of action, no more. One of a range available to us. Your suggestion turned out to be…poor value.'

'I'm not going to let you do this. I'll go to the paper with it.'

Pease looked almost sympathetic. 'It was only a week ago that you were entertaining the editor up there yourself.'

'Then I'll go national.'

'I'm afraid you're not in a position to go anywhere.'

Roger scanned the others seated around the table for some sign of hope. Malzeard stared back inscrutably. Maggie Roach looked across with concern and pity, as if seconds away from sectioning him. The deputy chief constable was peeking into a bag of complimentary gifts from PoundBlaster down by the side of his chair.

Roger locked in on Fitch, who was sitting back in his chair looking at him dispassionately. OK, maybe he felt let down by Spence and Roger. Maybe he felt betrayed that they'd turned his hard work into a freak show and made a mint doing it. But he knew Fitch wouldn't have it. The fact that he was even here proved Pease was scared of him. He wanted Fitch on board, had to have him on board. But Roger knew Fitch. This would turn the ASBU into a joke and that was the one thing he couldn't abide. Roger could sense that Fitch was revelling in the others' hypocrisy, just waiting for his moment. Fitch could blow the whole thing down.

'Boss?' pleaded Roger.

Pease looked across and raised both eyebrows, remembering something trivial. 'We haven't yet heard from Mr Fitch. Perhaps you would like to contribute.'

Fitch deliberately placed both hands behind his head and gave two small coughs.

'Antisocial behaviour.' he began, 'is the biggest single problem facing this local authority.' He ignored Maggie Roach's derisive tut. 'I've been fighting a losing battle for the last five years. But if we are prepared to let a small minority of people flout the conventions of what's acceptable out on our streets, then what does that say about us? So you've got a choice. You either try to stamp it out or you roll over and get trampled underfoot.'

'Isn't that rather apocalyptic?' asked the reverend, who wanted to develop his point. Fitch, however, cut him off with a flash of his hand.

'Let me say my fucking piece.' he snarled. 'All I want to say is that it's not theory to me or my team.' he said, gesturing to Roger. 'We see it day in, day out. We stare it down every day of the week. And what's our reward? You make us the niggers of Town Hall.'

They all drew breath, Maggie and Malzeard muttering their outrage. Roger knew that this was Fitch's two minutes in the sun, that for these few seconds he was untouchable, free to unburden himself of all the pent-up frustration he had stored from a thousand social policy meetings.

'Everybody wants their trash taken away, but nobody wants to get pally with the binmen. And you see what this work's done to them. It gets into you, gets inside you and churns you up. You don't need me to tell you that. Now I've got one member of staff lying in a coma and another who…well, you know what happened.'

Roger thought Fitch was overdoing it a bit but it didn't bother him. This was good stuff.

'But you know what?' he went on. 'I'm past caring. And the truth is, that if all these shitkickers are on one side of their fence doing their thing and I'm on the other, that's OK with me. Do your fucking worst.'

Everyone kept looking at him.

'Are you saying…?' Pease began.

'I'm saying, don't worry. I can turn a blind eye. And, yes, I'll send any ratboy worth his salt right your way.'

Pease waited a moment before speaking, consciously treading carefully. 'And the personal terms I've put forward?'

'I accept them.' Fitch sniffed. 'But I want the pension credits upfront. And index-linked.'

'Highly irregular.'

Fitch laughed. 'Irregular seems to be the order of the day, wouldn't you say?'

Roger was set to slump in his chair but saw that, with his parting shot, Fitch had clasped his briefcase shut and got up to leave. Roger started to follow him out.

'What was that?' he hissed at him when they made it to the top of the staircase, aware of but unconcerned by the presence of Maxine and Mason halfway up the stairs coming towards them.

Fitch turned on him. 'I know when I'm beaten. You started it, now live with it.'

'I don't want anything to do with it. What say I come back to the unit?'

Fitch just laughed. 'Hey, look, they can keep you on the payroll until hell freezes over but—' He thought of something. 'Anyway, we both know you can't leave. Not after what you did.'

Roger grabbed him by the arm. 'I was going through a difficult time. It was a personal thing. Spence turned it into the Show. That wasn't my idea. I just wanted to watch.'

Fitch looked at him closely, eyes narrowed.

'I don't think he remembers.' Maxine commented from beneath them. 'I don't think he—'

Fitch took his chance to scuttle down the stairs. 'I think you'd better tell him then, hadn't you?'

Roger gripped the banister tight, bent forward at the waist. 'Tell me what? Tell me what?'

Maxine and Mason shared a glance. Mason gave a little shrug.

'Well, basically…' he started.

'You killed Odom.' Maxine piled in. 'Totally.'

24

Roger sat on one of the settees, trying to make sense of what they'd just told him. Opposite him, Maxine and Mason sat quite close to each other. Roger wondered if there was something going on between them, then forgot about it.

At the larger table near the window, only Pease, Hendrick and Alan Uddin from Housing remained, poring over further income projections and cost analyses.

'Well.' Mason asked Roger. 'What do you make of the plan?'

'I want no part of it.'

Mason leaned forward. 'Come on, Rodge. You're already a part of it. You are it.' He put his hands out, showed Roger his palms. 'What else are you going to do?'

'I'm going to go back home. To my family.'

'You can't.'

'What are you talking about?'

'The Odom thing, Rodge. It's a big fucking thing, what you did.'

Roger licked his lips. He'd killed Odom. He'd found Odom in Maddy's room and he'd killed him. Apparently. It was too abstract a notion. What did it even mean? Odom was probably going to trundle into the room with a bad smell and a witless banality any second.

Mason came even closer. 'Rodge, you have to understand. You went…kind of berserk when you saw him. I mean, he was absolutely out of order, no question, but you took that fucking bat to him…'

'They had to scoop him up, Rodge.'

Roger's eyes flickered. He had a question.

'So who's doing his show now?'

They both laughed a little nervously.

'Thing is, Rodge, you're safe as long as you're here. With the coppers handling security now, not even McNally can muscle in. But if you set foot outside the Composers', you're a dead man. You knew Johnny was connected. Hard to believe, but he had friends. Spalding's just waiting for you to step off the estate…'

'When he gets off his drip.' added Maxine with a smile.

'Should have killed him as well.'

'Yeah.' nodded Maxine with a rueful laugh.

Mason went on. 'And, you know, you have to understand. There's more to it than that.'

Roger ran a hand through his greasy hair. 'More good news.'

'Part of the deal Pease made with the Old Bill is that you don't leave. Technically.' Mason told him, sitting back. 'Technically, what you did was murder.'

'He was trying to rape her! That's what you told me!'

Mason nodded slowly. 'That's obviously the way you saw it and you reacted accordingly. But the fact is that you made a Johnny smoothie out of him.'

'I don't remember.'

'No. You were kind of out of it.'

'I remember being at the hospital. How did I get there?'

'You carried Spence. Took the boat. Put the wind up Norman, you did. Then you must have grabbed a lift.'

'Or walked.' chimed in Maxine.

'Yeah.' agreed Mason, looking across at her, then at Roger. 'Or walked. The Old Bill don't want you out and about. Simple as that. Say what you like about Pease. He got them off your back.'

'Pease. For me?'

Mason made a little beckoning gesture over Roger's shoulder. The tall figure of Pease loomed. He stood for a second, then sat down next to Roger.

'We've explained the position.' Mason told him.

Pease gave Roger what was presumably his best effort at a sympathetic smile.

'You appreciate this is the best place for you.'

'I appreciate that I'm a prisoner here?'

Pease wore a pained expression.

'Not so much prisoner.' he said. 'More resident consultant. **Permanent** resident consultant.'

Back in his own room, Roger saw that they'd tidied up. Bed made, floor cleared. Roger found all his clothes cleaned and put away in the wardrobe he hadn't even known existed.

He looked around for the bat but it wasn't there.

He sat on the bed. The anglepoise rested on a small table at its head, illuminating the new bookcase, where his father's precious books had been placed, all standing in correct volume order.

He reached out and took one of the last ones down. Opening it, he turned to the title page. A small note facing it gave the name of the English publishers, adding that it had been produced in conjunction with the Russian Independent Institute of Social and National Problems (formerly the Institute of Marxism-Leninism), Moscow. Something about the name-change touched him. In the face of everything, they were still trying. They weren't accepting their fate.

He lay back on the bed and started to read.

25

Roger had to admit that the speed of work was extraordinary, particularly for someone used to watching the council in action. The building of the new health facility and attached drop-in social care centre on the west side of the estate away from the piazza, in front of Fairfax House, took little more than two weeks, assisted by the ten-foot fence that had been erected first and the troupe of security men and their massive Alsatians. The modest beginnings of the spire for Malzeard's new church could be seen peeping out over the newly reno-vated terrace of bungalows that comprised Purcell Mews. In the meantime, the reverend provided spiritual succour from a Portakabin around the back of Delius Grove. It was hard to argue with Pease's beaming assertions as to the effectiveness of private-sector involvement.

The transformation of Pandy's Handy into the country's first PoundBlaster Elite Convenience had been a straightfor-ward matter in comparison. Roger wondered where Pandy was now. Probably off with his cheque, setting up the cash and carry of his dreams on an industrial estate over the north side somewhere.

Around him there was sense of expectation in the air but it was muted, professional, businesslike – the air of a sure thing about to pass, not a thrilling risk. The cases of vintage Krug for the Show's gala reopening were being unpacked by the staff of HospInc, the firm that had beaten off stiff competition to win the private catering contract for Goossens at an improbably low price. Pease's oval strategy table had gone, replaced at the forefront of the third floor by a number of small tables arranged for viewing and dining, like a Vegas cabaret. A large bank of TV screens flanked the wall opposite the bar, all connected to CCTV cameras placed at various key points around the estate.

Roger's involvement had been minimal, although there had been moments when someone he didn't know would ask for confirmation of a trivial point, responding to his answer as if it was the insight of a Tibetan monk. He didn't welcome their attempts at inclusion. He merely watched, dead-eyed, his blood laced with guarana-infused Blast Bars and the new samples of Blam! vodka cup that had arrived and sat in the large glass-fronted chillers behind the expanded bar. Roger had tried all the flavours. He favoured apricot and passion fruit flavour. That one went best with his favourite Cool Thai Blast tortilla-style snacks, on which he largely subsisted. They were about the only thing he ate now. The sight of the bistro food that came up from the full-size kitchens now installed on the first floor made him nauseous. Some of the mostly foreign waiting staff were sitting, eating their pre-work meal and chatting quietly.

The day had been warm and clammy. It was the moment between late afternoon and evening that he always found melancholy on a summer's day. He stood at the window, an empty Blam! bottle dangling from the end of his index finger, so close to the glass that his breath appeared, misting the view. Occasionally he would let the back of his hand brush the small bulge emanating from his pocket, just to check that he still had the temazepam Dr Gilbert had given him. Sleep was a problem for Roger.

'Keeping watch?' asked a familiar if unwelcome voice behind him. Pease stepped up alongside. The councillor's awkward attempts at friendliness had been a feature of the last few days. He joined Roger in surveying the scene.

'Looking forward to it.' he said, breathing in hard through his nose. Half-statement, half-question.

Roger said nothing.

'You're happy with the arrangements?' Pease asked him.

Roger shrugged. 'Why ask me?'

'Because we value your advice. You invented the model.'

Roger splurted out a derisory laugh but Pease wanted to say his little piece.

'You can scoff if you like but you should realise what an enormous good you've done these people.'

'I've made them animals at the zoo.'

Pease shook his head.

'All this investment. They have *value* now. You've given them asset status. We need to take good care of them. And now they have some of the best health and social care anywhere in the country. You can take some of the credit for that.'

Roger laughed bitterly.

'Let me ask you something. You've built this complex to—' He waved a hand for inspiration.

'Protect our investment.' Pease reminded him.

'But you've got the police, the doctors, the yoghurt-knitters all looking after them, then who's going to try to stop them?'

'I'm not sure I understand.'

'They…*behave* to get a reaction.'

'I think we've established that they know they're being watched. There's always an audience, as you've proved.'

Roger felt tired. The effort of conversation had become alien to him.

'Yeah, but it's invisible. Up here, we might as well be a

CCTV camera. The whole reason their behaviour is antisocial is because it pisses other people off. Who are they going to be pissing off when everyone's next-door neighbour is as up for it as they are? Whose noses are they going to be rubbing it in?'

Pease's demeanour clouded over. 'What do you suggest?'

Roger said nothing but in truth he was remembering something. Remembering the two boys who'd approached Spence and him on the last night of the old Show.

Get down there.

Mix it up.

Roger looked down on the piazza, where the warm weather had encouraged some early revellers to lounge around, stoking themselves up with generous sundowners. Pease was right about one thing.

He did care. He wanted them all to be happy.

Pease shuffled on his feet. 'There's one other thing I wanted to talk to you about.'

'Huh?'

'We're no nearer reaching a conclusion. I think it's time we dealt with it head on.'

Roger knew what the ticklish subject was. He was suddenly keen to go back to his room and pick up his reading of Dad's books.

'The girl.' insisted Pease.

'What about her?'

'She'll have to return.'

Roger shook his head. 'In my role as consultant, I advise against it. I...fucking veto it.'

'She's not economically viable.'

'She helps around. Cleaning up.'

'We have contract cleaning staff.'

'Can't she help out behind the bar or something?'

Pease shook his head. 'These are legally licensed premises now.' he pointed out. 'Besides, we have important contingents coming tonight. It simply isn't appropriate.'

Roger knew who they were. Delegations from other surrounding authorities were on this evening's guest list. Pease
had a notion to start franchising the idea out until every city
had a Show of its own. Even Roger knew enough to know that
the natural resources required existed in abundance.

'The operation must appear completely legitimate.' Pease
went on. 'The sight of an underage girl, particularly one who
I have reason to believe has been stealing from us, anywhere
near the bar would give off entirely the wrong signal.'

Roger marvelled at Pease's capacity to take the fun out of
anything. He decided to try a different tack.

'She swore she'd blow our cover.'

Pease smiled thinly. 'I think we both know that won't make
much difference. You've just made the point that they don't
care about being watched. She's going back to her family.'

Pease made to walk off. Roger grabbed him by the lapels.

'Might as well put my new-found reputation for mindless
violence to good use.' he said, baring his teeth at Pease.

'Threatening me won't make any difference.'

'Think again.'

To his credit, Pease didn't flinch.

'No. I can't be a party to council-sanctioned kidnap.'

'Don't be fucking stupid.'

'Unlawful imprisonment.' insisted Pease.

'She doesn't want to go back.'

'I'm under police instructions.'

'She says she'll blow the Show.'

'The area has been sanitised. There's no way the news can
get out.'

Roger knew this was painfully true. The Composers' was
effectively a secure zone with police security stopping anybody
getting in from outside. Theoretically, people were free to
leave but, as the self-sufficiency of the new regime had crept

in, the numbers of those even contemplating popping out had dwindled to nothing. Similarly, research into mobile phone use undertaken by the police had shown that ninety-seven per cent of all calls were made to other numbers on the estate. The three per cent that had been lost by jamming the signal beyond the perimeter didn't seem to have caused any undue perturbation out on the streets. The ongoing work on the site had been used as a front to permanently disable the small number of land lines that still existed. The three full-time staff hired to filter incoming and outgoing post had quickly had their number reduced to one when the true paucity of letter-writing had been revealed. With so little to do, the remaining mail monitor was also given the job of rooting out unnecessary postal distractions. The total absence of circulars and junk mail was just another improvement in the quality of life that every citizen of the Composers' unwittingly benefited from. More than half of the postal traffic came in the form of approved purchases from CostBlast TV.

Roger dropped his hands. 'She's not going back.' he said, trying to make it sound like the last word. Dad's books had persuaded him there was hope. There had to be the hope of escape for someone. 'She's not going back.'

'She must.'

'Why?'

Pease gestured to the bank of TV screens nearby, reached for the remote that sat in a bracket attached to the wall.

'Because we want to see what happens when she does. Maybe I forgot to mention. It's one of our gala-night features.'

The TV screens all snapped images at the same time to reveal one giant shot of Mrs Marsh, Maddy's mother, sprawled backwards on her settee nursing a can of PoundBlaster Premium Brew and sucking hard on a pipe attached to a plastic bag.

'You're in their homes.' Roger said, awe-struck.

'We agreed this would be more cost effective than a retractable roof over the piazza in case of bad weather.'

'Spence was always worried about it raining.' Roger said dreamily.

'Also offers an action replay facility for anything worth seeing again. Potential home video market.' he added almost apologetically. He extinguished the screens and replaced the remote, seeking out Roger's undivided attention.

'The only reason I've let her stay until now is because we were saving her for tonight.' A hint of distaste crossed his mouth. He paused, then spoke again, more slowly. 'Whatever happens.' he said, 'she leaves here tonight.'

Roger picked up on the change in language. 'But that's different. That's different from saying she has to go back down there.'

'Let me put it this way. She goes back down there tonight…unless…'

'Unless what?'

'We reopen tonight. You understand we need something to mark the occasion. Something special.'

'What do you want to see out there?'

Uncharacteristically, Pease put his hands in his pockets. 'That's your area. I defer to you in programming matters. But if you can promise me something…memorable, maybe we can reach a compromise.'

He left, leaving Roger staring at the blank screens. The bottle of temazepam in his pocket rattled as he transferred his weight from one leg to the other. It was telling him something.

He walked quickly down to the second floor and, making sure he wasn't seen, quietly entered the locker room for the catering staff. At this hour, with preparations in full swing, virtually all the personnel had come in, and along one wall a row of hooks was supporting dozens of coats. Once sure he was alone, Roger began rifling through them. He was squeezing the pocket of the fourth one when he felt the reassuring weight of a mobile phone. He pulled it out and was gratified to see it was switched on.

He left the room and headed for the main internal staircase, the one that ran like a corkscrew around the lift shaft.

He started up.

It took him half an hour to reach the roof. The very design faults that had made so many lives a misery in Goossens' history now stood him in good stead in avoiding the personnel of the Show as they crept ever up the building. Sneaking outside on the sixth floor, he had used the Byzantine external stairways so beloved of burglars and drug-dealers, only having to return within for the last two flights. He'd had to kick in an old rusty padlock to get out on to the roof, but once up there he wondered why he hadn't made the pilgrimage to the summit before. Up here, with the strong breeze and the whole city laid out before him, the traffic moving like blood through the streets, he was overwhelmed with a sense of hope. Even the aberrations of Odom that were visible to the naked eye seemed to fit into some greater organic design. Out there, only good things could happen. He resolved to act once more.

He'd been present when the scheme to block the mobile phone signal had been explained. A network of interceptors had been placed around the estate not allowing calls to be received or passed out. But with the mobile deemed to be the single piece of equipment the residents could least survive without, a leading telecoms company had joined the Private Finance Initiative and stumped up for the Composers' to have its own cellular exchange and every resident to get a new, free phone. They could call each other until they were hoarse and never receive a bill. About the only thing that Roger had remembered was about the range of the jamming zone. Pease's innate economic instincts had led to the conclusion that the field needed to be only a hundred feet high, some way higher than the tallest populated building on the estate. Goossens, of course, stretched way higher than any other building but that didn't matter because it wasn't populated, was it?

And up here the signal was strong. Almost laughing with excitement, he dialled a number he still remembered, one from another life.

26

He found Maddy in his room, lying on his bed, watching CostBlast, the volume of Marx on the floor where she'd pushed it off the bed.

He smiled at her and offered her one of the two bottles of cherry-and-almond-flavoured Blam! he was carrying. She looked at him with a touch of suspicion.

'What about the baby?' she asked.

'Live a little.' he said, taking a swig of the purple syrup. 'One won't do any harm.'

She took the bottle and he watched her neck half of it. After a few minutes the temazepam he'd put in it had kicked in and she lay asleep, her head lolled to the side, a thin streak of vermilion dribble trickling down the pillow.

He looked outside to check if it was all clear. His forced relocation to the second floor was a big help as it meant he didn't have to go past the nerve centre upstairs on his way down with her. Contact with the kitchens below was through an internal lift system converted from the old laundry chutes, so there wasn't much traffic that way, especially as punters were now being brought up in the building's main elevators, turd-free and running like clockwork now.

He slung Maddy over his shoulder and headed out,

stopping in his tracks a couple of times at a sound from above. But he got to the stairs OK and tripped down two flights to the old familiar door just as her weight became too much and he had to let her down. Slumped against the door in leaden sleep, Maddy still had an air of innocence about her. Doing the right thing, he repeated to himself as, after a short break, he bent down to haul her back up in a fireman's lift.

The short trip from the back of Goossens to the jetty was, he knew, the most dangerous part of the journey, even though the covered walkway had been extended to cover most of the way. If there was anyone coming towards him or in there, putting finishing touches to it before tonight, then he was screwed. But he was getting lucky. So lucky that he had to be doing the right thing.

Unseen, he made it to the jetty, rebuilt and doubled in size now. Adjacent to it, stern facing him, the barge sat on the water. Sweating hard and aware of his own panting as if it were the breath of a rhino he was lying in bed next to, Roger could make out the back of Norman's head in the cockpit, reading a newspaper. With the girl still bent over him, he carefully stepped on to the boat's rear, lowered her to the deck and, crouching down, moved himself around, unzipping his jacket pocket and pulling out the empty Blam! bottle. With a sudden lunge, he jumped in on Norman.

'Take us to the pick-up.' he told him.

Norman seemed unperturbed.

'What are you going to do with that?' he wanted to know, looking down at the bottle.

Roger lifted it, as if to smash the neck on the counter top. 'I'll glass you.'

Norman rolled his eyes. 'Away wich'ya, you daft sod. Put the fecking thing down. I'll take you where you want to go.'

Roger stood the bottle on the counter.

'Haven't seen you for a while.' Norman said, blinking

slowly. 'Be'Jesus, but you've lost a fucking ton of weight.'

'Can we just go!'

'All right, all right. Keep your decorum.'

He started the engines and skilfully slid the boat in a forward direction.

'I'd heard you weren't supposed to be leaving.'

Roger stared ahead, watching the water as they chugged through it. 'I'm not leaving.'

'So what are we doing?'

'I said I'm not leaving.'

Norman's face clouded then cleared. 'OK, I get you.' He threw a look over his shoulder. 'So where is she?'

'Out the back. Asleep.'

Norman nodded. Roger felt there was judgement in his silence.

'I'm doing the right thing.' he said.

'Whatever you say, squire. I'm just the ferryman. One thing, though.' he said, reaching up to a shelf above his head and pulling out a packet of cigarettes, extracting one with his mouth. 'If they ask, I'll have to tell them that you threatened to kill me.'

Roger looked up at him questioningly.

'Oh yeah.' said Norman, lighting up with pleasure. 'I saw what you done to that other feller. They won't doubt it. That's for sure.'

Dennis Priest was standing next to his old Astra, in a car coat and a flat cap, his reading glasses hanging around his neck on a chain. The pick-up point wasn't much changed from the last time Roger had seen it, although they had built a proper ramp, painted out some proper car-parking spaces and put up a sign advertising the Leisure and Amenities Department of the council, in collaboration with PoundBlaster.

As Norman expertly slowed and turned the boat, Roger

picked up Maddy, who let out a low groan, in his arms and stepped off towards Dennis.

'Open the car.' he instructed him.

He slid her on to the back seat and closed the door.

'What happened to her?' Dennis asked.

'They drugged her. You have to get her away.'

Dennis left it there. He had other things on his mind.

'Where've you been?' he wanted to know.

'I can't tell you that, Dennis.'

'I bloody well want to know.'

'Ask Fitch.'

'Fitch? He spends all day down the bloody pub. The unit's gone to pieces. I'm barely able to maintain any kind of cohesive policy. We're being so ineffective that people have just stopped making any complaints about their neighbours.'

'That a fact?' Roger said, looking down the track that led out towards a previous existence he dimly recalled.

'When are you coming back?' Dennis asked. 'When are you all coming back?'

Roger was touched by his tone, almost on the verge of tears, it sounded like. He gave Priest a quick smile, then gestured to the car.

'Take care of her.' he said, moving back towards the boat. 'Favour to me.'

Dennis nodded sadly. 'I've got her booked into temporary accommodation for tonight. The Refuge are taking her in tomorrow. They've placed her on their parent education watchlist and she's going to do mornings at a community college over Gatford way. They specialise in teaching literacy.' He patted Roger on the back. 'I've alerted Social Services and they're going to do a fostering evaluation, for when the baby's born. It's all in hand. You've done the right thing.'

On the boat trip back to the Composers', Roger wondered if he hadn't made a terrible mistake.

When they reached the jetty alongside Goossens, Norman didn't bother to moor up.

'Got to turn her straight around, pick up the first customers.' he explained as Roger jumped off. 'How long before they find out she's gone, you reckon?'

Roger shrugged. 'Doesn't matter. Where she's gone, there's no getting her back.'

He turned to leave but Norman hollered.

'Got something of yours here.' he said and flung an object that Roger caught in both hands.

His bat.

'Pease told me to give it to you if I saw you. I gave it a wash.'

Roger nodded his thanks.

'I was thinking about something I said to you.' said the bargeman, picking up a thick rope and beginning to roll it around his fist and elbow. 'About scraping the shit off. Sometimes, you know, you can scrape the shit off something and then not like what you find underneath. Don't get me wrong. I liked working for you and Spence. But now…I was happy selling the *Big Issue*. Maybe wasn't much good at it, but I liked the company in that job, you know what I mean? I think I might go back into that game.'

27

Roger bided his time, sitting on an abandoned couch in front of the locked gate that led out on to the towpath. The sun started its descent before him, and he closed his eyes at its warm touch on the taut skin around his cheeks. He could clearly hear the sound of the barge as it returned and the low but excited babble of the first batch of gala-night guests. He gave it three trips before his thirst got the better of him and he rose, heading off towards the heart of the estate.

The clatter of the aluminium bat on the asphalt beneath him announced him to the good crowd out on the piazza as he made a straight diagonal from where he had emerged to what would always be Pandy's Handy, as far as he was concerned, whatever the fucking sign out front said. He knew that Pease would be watching him from above, dimly appreciated that there was an inevitability about his presence down here. And a correctness.

That he was fulfilling his half of the bargain.

They watched him as he walked among them, cans and bottles scattered at their feet. He fought his own sense of intimidation at their physical reality, at their actual size. Not that they were larger than any other humans he had known. Simply that he had been watching so long from a distance that he had reduced them in his mind to the size of small gibbons, or large marmosets. The ones who weren't noticeably fat were noticeably lean, either very fit or very ill. Something in their general demeanour made the clothes they wore, although all in the 'leisurewear' category, look distinctly uncomfortable. Nominally at relaxation, they radiated an irritable energy. The atmosphere was one of concentration, hovering on the point between alertness and fear.

One or two of the men who were seated on the edge of the planters stood, arms folded across their bare torsos, watching him dead-eyed and open-mouthed. A few jabbering, repetitive conversations were interrupted by the scraping noise of the bat on the ground. He left some whispers or grunted questions in his wake, but gradually silence fell around him until it was only the voice of the bat that resonated. With every step he felt a little stronger, and he walked a little taller until he stood at the door to the shop.

He waited a second before they buzzed him in.

A shock of cold went through him as he entered and the sharpness of the neon lighting forced him to close his eyes.

An amplified voice called to him. 'COULD YOU PUT THE BAT DOWN, PLEASE, SIR.'

He bent down and laid it on the floor. Opening his eyes gradually, he saw three banks of chiller cabinets stretch the entire length of the shop, each one five feet high and full to capacity with bottles and cans: Blam! in all its myriad varieties, BreezeBlasts (three new flavours to try), LifeBlast Regular, HealthBlast Caffeine Fix, Surge Cola Classic, Surge Power Formula, Red Blast Regular, Red Blast!, Red Alert, GameBlast Sports Supplement in Citrus Spurt, Berry Burst and Grape Gush. Further on, the four-litre plastic flagons of cider, the lagers and boxes of white wine. Roger grabbed two cold bottles of his favoured Blam! and chugged half of one down before continuing his look around.

On both sides of the next two lanes, the rest of the booze. An awesome selection of wines and spirits, all bearing the corporate mark. Roger walked and scanned the rows, impressed that PoundBlaster had its own-brand low-fat advocaat line. But who would fail to be impressed by this…this paradise?

On the final two aisles, it was sweets and crisps, enough for all.

Roger carried on to the back of the store, where two young black men sat at a counter behind a sheet of glass with a few grilles at the bottom for exchange. They both wore white polo shirts, red baseball caps and electronic headsets. The fags, thousands of packets, were behind them. A sign hung above them, supported by metal chains attached to the ceiling.

UNDER 16 – NO TOBACCO
UNDER 18 – NO ALCOHOL

'How much?' Roger asked, holding aloft the bottles.

They looked at each other.

'Nothing, mate.'

Roger nodded, stuck out his bottom lip. 'I knew the bloke who used to own this store.'

'Nice for you.'

He paused.

'I need something else.'

'Oh yeah?'

'Yeah.'

'What sort of thing, exactly?'

'Something to pep me up, you know.' Roger said with a sniff.

'Pep you up?'

'Yeah, you know, put a little fire under me. I have to, you know, perform.'

One of them gave a sullen nod and produced a small plastic bag containing two red pills. 'These should do you.' he said, passing them through. 'Want anything to calm you down, for after?'

Roger shook his head, threw the two pills into his mouth and washed them down with Blam!

'Thanks.' he said and headed to the door. He picked up the bat and they buzzed him out.

The sultry evening reclaimed him and he felt the first swinging kick off the pills. Straight in there, not like the hit-and-miss rubbish Darren from Housing used to give him. A surge of energy coursed his veins. Jets fired within him. He felt a buzz of transformation in his forehead, as if he were about to sprout horns.

The pack had imperceptibly approached and turned to face him while he had been inside. From the front, a skeletal youth with a New York Mets baseball cap and a wad of cotton wool taped over one of his eyes came forward and got close. Very close.

'Here, mate.' he said, hopping from one foot to the other. 'Here, mate, you all right? You all right? How you doing? You all right, all right, all right?' He repeated himself, as if all that his emaciated frame contained was his own echo.

Roger moved but the boy went with him, predicting each step like a shadow. His one good eye was one giant pupil, like a black billiard ball rolling on its axis inside his head.

'How you doing? You doing all right? Here, mate, mate, mate…'

Roger tried to brush past him and walk towards the centre of the group.

'I'll tell you what it is, mate. Thing is.' he giggled, 'I'm off me face here. I'm as bollocksed out as fuck and…mate, have you got any bus fare so I can buy fags, like fags, fags, fags?'

Roger looked down. ''S all free, mate.' he said.

The boy shook his head. 'Thing is, I reckon I must have whited about seven times. Look at me eye. I'm total space cadet, man, you with me? All I'm after is a bit of bus fare.' He laughed again. 'Have you got summat I can nick off you, off you?'

Roger felt another, more powerful surge off the drugs and he lunged out, almost involuntarily, brushing the ratboy off and sending him to the floor. He threw up his head and began to shout.

'I want you to listen to me!' he summoned them, hearing his own voice as if he was under water. 'Just stop what you're doing for a minute and listen to me!'

Most of them, but not all, looked. Ratboy dragged himself to his feet and resumed his invasion of Roger's personal space.

'What you fucking do that for, dickhead?' he spat. 'Give us your fucking watch! Dickhead! Fucking gizzit! Gizzit! Gizzit!'

Roger raised the bat in his left hand as another huge narcotic shiver went through him. The boy swayed on his heels to avoid its arc as Roger roared on.

'Pay attention! Listen to me.' he insisted. 'You are all being watched. They're all up there, watching what you do.' He pointed the barrel of the bat straight up at Goossens and the third floor. 'They're up there, behind the glass, watching, drinking and eating. Eating and drinking while you…suffer grievous exploitation.'

He realised they were starting to crowd in. *Yes*, he thought. *They're listening!* No doubt that, as they neared, there was an intense look in their eyes. Manic almost. Roger felt intense panic, then a sudden sense of relaxation as another, stronger Roger took over, speaking freely. The words emerging were words he had read. Words from the red books handed down to him by his father.

'You, the instruments of production…'

'Gizzus yer fucking watch…'

236

'…appendages of the machine…'

'…I want it, dickhead…'

Roger began undoing his watchstrap.

'…smash these feudal ties…' he insisted.

The one-eyed boy put out his hand. 'Gizzit! Or I'll chin ya.'

Roger dropped it into his palm. 'All property is theft.' he explained.

'What else you got?'

The crowd were very near, close to swallowing him up.

'Fucking get him!'

Roger raised the bat. 'You have nothing to lose…'

The first blow, when it came, was delivered to the back of his head, from an object thrown at him. Then came another, a kick this time, aimed hard at the back of his legs. He half-buckled and more rough contact sent him down on to his knees. He saw the pristine trainer coming as it was planted heavily on his chest, forcing him down on his back. As he fell, Roger held the bat tight to him and closed his eyes.

He just managed to roll over as the beating began in earnest.

The moments of contact, as they rained in on him, were painful but each one seemed to charge him with energy. The pain that flared up in their aftermath was not the self-pitying ache he might have feared but a kind of awakening, a new awareness of his own physicality.

He realised that he was undergoing a rite. Each strike felt like a welcome. When they were finished with him, he knew he would truly belong.

A friendly boot to the head lulled him quickly to sleep.

EPILOGUE

Since one portion of value, as well as the price of production, is an actually given constant, namely the cost price, representing the capital = k used up in production, the difference consists in the other, the variable portion, the surplus value, which equals p, the profit, in the price of production, i.e. equals the total surplus value calculated on the social capital and on every individual capital as an aliquot part of the social capital; but which in the value of commodities equals the actual surplus value created by this particular capital, and forms an integral part of the commodity values produced by this capital. If the value of commodities is higher than their price of production, then the price of production = k + p, and the value = k + p + d, so that p + d = the surplus value contained therein. The difference between the value and the price of production, therefore, = d, the excess of surplus value created by this capital over the surplus value allocated to it through the general rate of profit.

Roger closed the book gently and returned the volume to its correct place in the long red sequence, then let his finger trace the length of one of the shelves, pleased by the undulations of each spine as it rose and fell.

He sat in the sole chair, opposite the window, underneath the reading lamp that sat on the bookcase. The bed was in the same room, a bare mattress and a sleeping bag on top. The flat they'd given him, on the second floor of Bax Villas, had two bedrooms, but he preferred to have everything in one room. They'd offered him any number of luxuries but he declined. He rarely visited the kitchen in the flat except to grab a Blast Energy Bar from the cupboard or a can of Surge from the fridge.

He consulted the clock on his complimentary third-generation WAP phone with MP3, camera and video-streaming functions. There were hundreds of other things it could do, but Roger only ever used it to tell the time, as he no longer had a watch.

It was nearly nine and the late summer light outside was beginning to dim.

Not long now.

He raised his arms and stretched. There was still an ache in the shoulder he had dislocated a fortnight or so ago but the medical staff had been as excellent as ever, as they had been ever since he had been admitted following his initiatory beating. As a result of it, he suffered from a slight deafness in one ear and persistent aches in his left arm and leg, which had both been broken. The headaches were largely a thing of the past following Dr Gilbert's increase in his dosage. Roger didn't like to make a fuss. After all, he wasn't the only one out there on the front line every night. But he was grateful for the twice-weekly check-ups that he, like most on the Composers', received, although, as he often pointed out, healthcare free at the point of the need was a fundamental human right. Article Number Two, he vaguely remembered from somewhere.

Outside evening time, he generally kept himself to himself. He read and reread the books and occasionally ventured to see Malzeard and discuss certain aspects of Marxist thinking from across the reinforced glass of his office. He had soon realised that he was way ahead of the reverend, whose socialist principles were moribund, mired in the swamp of moral orthodoxy. There were times when Roger even thought he detected distaste at Roger's means of self-expression. Roger sometimes had to remind Malzeard that he was no more than a bourgeois lackey, beholden to the captains of industry. After all, Roger knew.

That usually shut him up.

Roger checked the time again. Time to get ready.

He reached across and picked up the baseball bat that stood leaning where the bookcase met the wall. He drew it to him, resting it across his lap and studying the array of dents and marks it bore, checking out its grooves and bumps with his thumb. A story in every one, he thought, allowing himself the smallest of smiles. He wondered, as he always did around this time, who would be emerging from down the shaft tonight, wearing the helmets and body armour the capitalists gave their side for the fray. Perhaps someone he had met on the piazza already, back for more. Or perhaps new candidates for conversion.

From the start, Roger had decided that he wasn't going to let them just watch.

The two boys on the stag night didn't realise it but it was they who'd sowed the seeds of protest in Roger's mind. The Show would no longer be for spectators. It would become a participation sport. Actions had to speak louder than words. They'd taught him that on his first night on the piazza. That was why, after recovering, he'd stood for the first three nights as a Composers' resident, standing alone underneath Goossens, slapping his bat on the concrete piazza and challenging the first of them to come down. He knew they couldn't resist. And he knew his enemy. He knew Pease would see the business sense in it. *Your chance to take part in a pitched battle on the piazza every night. Form a queue here…*

Spence and Roger had taken the Show as spectacle as far as it could go. If the capitalists wanted action now, they'd have to come down and get it for themselves. But they were playing into Roger's hands and the hands of everyone who called the Composers' home. He knew that once they'd come out from behind the black glass on the third floor, once they'd been lured down, once they'd tasted that freedom, it would rub off on them. They'd be back again and again, addicted to it, until they saw the light and became free men themselves. Just like Roger.

Roger stood. He picked up the two red pills he'd earlier placed on the bookcase, put them in his mouth and washed them down with the dregs of his seventh, maybe eighth Blam! of the day.

He opened the door to his flat and, stepping out on to the walkway, sensed the buzz of expectation that swelled up across the Composers' at this time every night.

He wished his dad could see him, heading out into the certainty of struggle.

Here there was permanent revolution.

Every night. Nine o'clock sharp.

Also Published by Serpent' Tail

Refusal Shoes
Tony Saint

Immigration Officer Henry Brinks likes to keep out of
trouble, but when he unwittingly stumbles onto a scam
to smuggle Chinese crooks into the country he discovers
that his colleagues are the last people to turn to. *Refusal
Shoes* is a blackly comic novel based on the author's
years of working for the Immigration Service. Set in
the Immigration Office of a major UK airport populated by a group of idiosyncratic, superbly drawn
characters, *Refusal Shoes* offers an insider's view into the
secretive and surreal world of passport control.

If you've ever been on the receiving end of an immigration officer, know someone who has, or are just
curious about what they can (and do) get away with,
then you must read this hilarious novel. Once you have,
going through passport control will never be quite the
same again!

'A gloriously entertaining satirical thriller' *Guardian*

'So successful in its depiction of the flickering-fluorescent petty-politicking of immigration officers — where
productivity is measured in 'refused leave to enter'
stamps — that you almost start worrying whether your
own papers are in order' **Tony White**

'A high-farce, fast and funny debut thriller…When you take this book on holiday, get someone to bring it back for you through customs' **Arnold Brown**

'A brutally funny first novel which refuses to pull any punches' **Ben Richards**

'*Refusal Shoes* comes on like a cross between Airport and *League of Gentlemen*… Saint writes some very funny dialogue and offers sharp observation' ***Independent on Sunday***

'A gruesomely comic account of an immigration service… *Refusal Shoes* brings a new perspective to a big current topic while also being highly entertaining' ***Daily Telegraph***

'*Refusal Shoes* scores black comedy points for its portrayal of Henry's workmates as risibly inadequate specimens of inhumanity. Their goonishly casual, institutionalised racism and crackhanded attempts at corruption make for a piquant entertainment. In a climate in which asylum seekers are scapegoated by the press, Saint's insider knowledge gives this comedy a potent topical tang' ***Metro London***

'*Refusal Shoes* is an amusing satirical thriller that provides an eye-popping glimpse behind the immigration desks at Heathrow. It shocks in more ways that one' ***Sunday Telegraph***

Blag
Tony Saint

Harry Verma – small-time immigration solicitor, nursing a sick father and a gambling habit – has taken to pulling more than just the odd legal aid fraud to help pay his unpredictable creditors. Sean Carlisle – enforcement officer, collaring illegal immigrants for a living – is self-destructing. Booze, pills and bending the law to get results are all taking their toll on his judgement.

Two men on opposite sides of a blurred line have more in common than they think. When a runaway Asian bride, her corrupt father-in-law and a psychotic Glaswegian immigration officer bring them inexorably together, Harry and Sean have little choice but to team up for the blag of their lives.

'The absurdity and petty injustices brought Kingsley Amis to mind' *Daily Telegraph*

'The novel is an eye-opener' *Uncut*

'[a] grimly amusing tale… what makes it enjoyable (and slightly worrying) is that it's not that far-fetched' *Metro London*

'Like the novels of Magnus Mills and the TV work of Ricky Gervais and the *League of Gentlemen* crew, this is a work in the emerging school of the new absurd, the British banal – morally accurate, spiritually depressing and vastly readable' *Big Issue in the North* (**4-star review**)

We Need to Talk About Kevin
Lionel Shriver
Winner of the 2005 Orange Prize for Fiction

Two years ago, Eva Khatchadourian's son, Kevin, murdered seven of his fellow high-school students, a cafeteria worker, and a popular algebra teacher. Because he was only fifteen at the time of the killings, he received a lenient sentence and is now in a prison for young offenders in upstate New York. Telling the story of Kevin's upbringing, Eva addresses herself to her estranged husband through a series of letters. Fearing that her own shortcomings may have shaped what her son has become, she confesses to a deep, long-standing ambivalence about both motherhood in general and Kevin in particular. How much is her fault?

Lionel Shriver tells a compelling, absorbing, and resonant story while framing these horrifying tableaux of teenage carnage as metaphors for the larger tragedy - the tragedy of a country where everything works, nobody starves, and anything can be bought but a sense of purpose.

'An awesomely smart, stylish and pitiless achievement…
Franz Kafka wrote that a book should be the ice-pick that breaks open the frozen seas inside us, because the books that make us happy we could have written ourselves. With *We Need to Talk About Kevin*, Shriver has wielded Kafka's axe with devastating force' ***Independent***

'Pitch-perfect, devastating and utterly convincing' **Geoff Dyer**

'My beach novel of choice is Lionel Shriver's book *We Need to Talk About Kevin* – a tense account of a mother who gives birth to a child she unapologetically dislikes from the start, and who grows up to be a teenage mass murderer – although the book serves only to reinforce what I already knew: that it is unreasonable, not to say unnatural, for adults to be expected to like all children just because they are small' ***Guardian***

'One of the most striking works of fiction to be published this year. It is *Desperate Housewives* as written by Euripides… A powerful, gripping and original meditation on evil' ***New Statesman***

'This startling shocker strips bare motherhood… the most remarkable Orange prize victor so far' **Polly Toynbee,** ***Guardian Weekly***

'At a time when fiction by women has been criticized for its dull domesticity, here is a fierce challenge of a novel by a woman that forces the reader to confront assumptions about love and parenting, about how and why we apportion blame, about crime and punishment, forgiveness and redemption and, perhaps most significantly, about how we can manage when the answer to the question why? is either too complex for human comprehension, or simply non-existent' ***Independent***

'Harrowing, tense and thought-provoking, this is a vocal challenge to every accepted parenting manual you've ever read' **Andrew Morrod,** ***Daily Mail***

Double Fault
Lionel Shriver

'Love me, love my game' says twenty-three year-old Willy Novinsky. Ever since she picked up a racquet at the age of four, tennis has been Willy's one love, until the day she meets Eric Oberdorf. She's a middle-ranked professional tennis player and he's a Princeton graduate who took up playing tennis at the age of eighteen. Low-ranked but untested, Eric, too, aims to make his mark on the international tennis circuit. Willy beholds compatibility spiced with friendly rivalry, and discovers her first passion outside a tennis court. They marry.

Married life starts well but animated shop talk and blissful love-making soon give way to full-tilt competition over who can rise to the top first. Driven and gifted, Willy maintains the lead until she severs her knee ligaments in a devastating spill. As Willy recuperates, her ranking plummets whilst her husband's climbs, until he is eventually playing in the US Open. Anguished at falling short of her lifelong dream and resentful of her husband's success, Willy slides irresistibly toward the first quiet tragedy of her young life.

Lionel Shriver's seventh novel, *We Need to Talk About Kevin*, won the 2005 Orange Prize. Her other novels are: *A Perfectly Good Family*, *Game Control*, *Ordinary Decent Criminals*, *Checker and the Derailleurs* and *The Female of the Species*. She has also written for the Guardian, Financial Times, Wall Street Journal, and the Economist. She lives in London.